PEROXIDE HOMICIDE

PEROXIDE HOMICIDE

MATTHEW MALEKOS

ROBERT HALE · LONDON

© Matthew Malekos 2013
First published in Great Britain 2013

ISBN 978-0-7198-0799-2

Robert Hale Limited
Clerkenwell House
Clerkenwell Green
London EC1R 0HT

www.halebooks.com

2 4 6 8 10 9 7 5 3 1

Typeset in New Century Schoolbook
Printed by MPG Printgroup, UK

DEDICATION

For my mother: a woman of indeterminable inner
strength and determination. With thanks also to D.M.
who when I say *'Come What May'* will know exactly what
I mean, and to my good friend Mr Nilsen, for persevering
with my inquisitiveness for the past fifteen years.

Thanks to all at Robert Hale Ltd for believing that
Peroxide Homicide had the potential to reach the pages
of this book.

Chapter One

**Saturday 8 October, 6 p.m.,
Central Manchester Mortuary**

It might have been that the tiredness, which had been building steadily throughout the day after the long night before, blurred the edges of Dr Karen Laos's vision as she stood looking through the doorway of the entrance to the mortuary, over which she had presided as the on-call pathologist for a fifteen-hour stretch.

It very likely *was* tiredness but it might also have been that the sheer strain of her eventful night was taking its toll on her. As she stood motionless, contemplating the day's events, Dr Laos failed to notice the sound of her coffee cup overflowing in the vending machine.

'Damn it!' she cursed, hurrying into animated action and taking a tissue from her pocket, talking to no one in particular. As she pushed the outdated *on-off* switch to stop the flow of premixed coffee and milk, she fleetingly thought about the number of requests she and her staff had made to management for a new vending machine to be installed.

Budgets, they had reminded her. A touch of irritability

grew in the pit of her stomach as she wiped the remaining droplets of overspill that ran down the side of her cup onto her now saturated tissue.

The call had seemed ordinary enough for a weekend night in Manchester's inner-city area. Dr Laos had worked this beat for more than a decade, her personal life having been slowly eroded over the years. Her mobile phone had buzzed at 3 a.m. from the top of her bedside dressing table, and at first she had failed to recognize the caller identity that was to propel her into a night the like of which she had known only once before, in the early years of her career – six long years ago.

Dr Laos prided herself on being considered – by her colleagues and the city's leading murder squad – as the best pathologist working in forensics. Only on this occasion her sense of self-confidence in her ability to complete the task at hand felt severely tested, as it had been all those years ago when she first failed to solve the case of a particularly gruesome murder.

The person responsible for the crime had never been identified, and the process of identifying the victim had taken all of a year to complete, due to the extent of ante-mortem torture that had been inflicted. The victim: *case number AA-262*, she thought, feeling a shudder of guilt. Quickly she replaced this nondescript title with one that she felt was more humane: *the wounded child.*

For some reason, Dr Laos found that she was unwilling to say the victim's name in her mind. She hadn't been the only pathologist involved in that case – her predecessor had taken the lead – but she still felt the burden of guilt.

Failed. The word struck deep within her thoughts as she now cast her mind back over the years, trying to remember the face of Detective Inspector James Roberts. His call to her mobile in the early hours had been the first she had heard from him since that long-ago unsolved case. That it came at 3 a.m. should have justified her inability to immediately place him, but for some reason, on this occasion, it did not.

Maybe she had purposely forgotten his face, his stature. She had met him briefly during the process of investigating the murder of *the wounded child*, but his speciality lay outside the remit of the mainstream murder squad: this cop was in another league, a chillingly different type altogether. He investigated child homicide and sexual offences against minors. Maybe, she told herself, this was why she found the thought of what he represented and the thought of what the latest body lying on the slab in the mortuary might represent so disturbing. Roberts was also elusive, thinly spread across the region, and had gained a reputation as an excellent psychological profiler. As such thoughts crossed Dr Laos's mind, she failed to notice her assistant, Maxwell, approaching.

Maxwell, at twenty-seven years old, fifteen years her junior, had an energy about him that Dr Laos liked and respected; he also had willpower, and she often felt slightly jealous of his ability to switch off at even the darkest of moments. She didn't consider herself burnt out but she certainly thought often about the changes she had noticed in her personality since she had first started her career.

She was dedicated to the point of not being able to live the relatively normal life that Maxwell had outside of his work. He had friends, he had a relationship; these were things that Karen Laos knew she had forfeited in order to be the best forensic pathologist she could possibly become.

'Dr Laos!' called Maxwell as he approached from the entrance of the mortuary.

Startled back to reality, she replied, 'Maxwell, yes? What can I do for you?' She noticed that Maxwell was looking at her with concern.

'I'm just checking to see how you are. It's been thirty minutes since you came for your coffee.'

'Thirty minutes? I'm sorry, I seem to have lost track of time,' she said apologetically. 'This damn coffee machine has been playing up again.'

Maxwell was quick to clock the distant expression in his superior's eyes and the unconvincing tone of her speech, but sensible enough to make light of the situation, quipping back, 'Tell me about it. I'm often driven to the point of fury with that machine.'

He grinned as he spoke, his smile magnified by his six-foot-four-inch frame as he hovered over her. Karen Laos knew that her white lie about the coffee machine had not fooled Maxwell. He had also shown the strain of today's events in his own way. *Who wouldn't want some reprieve from the police constables and crime scene unit, who had been under their feet all day?*

Knowing she had been caught off-guard, Dr Laos decided to get back to work. She shared an unspoken understanding with her assistant, which meant that neither had to articulate their feelings to the other. She was saved the need to acknowledge her moments of vulnerability and he knew how to make such moments easier for her to manage. This was an act that Maxwell had learned early on in his work with Dr Laos. It was one that she had fully recognized from day one, and by now she had perfected her own part in the exchange.

They walked back along the corridor and through the entrance into the mortuary, Dr Laos keeping two steps ahead of Maxwell's pace but occasionally turning to speak to him about the work at hand.

Stopping a few yards into the lobby of the mortuary, she turned to face her assistant and said, 'Maxwell, it's been a long day, and no doubt the next few days will be the same. Why don't you go home and get some rest? We both have to be back here first thing tomorrow morning.'

Maxwell paused momentarily, before concurring.

'I'm not the only one who should be heading home, Dr Laos. You too need your sleep. Have you heard from Detective Roberts since this morning?'

'Yes, Maxwell, I have. The inspector's been delayed but he'll be here tomorrow morning at 8 a.m. and he'll be expecting our initial findings.'

Maxwell studied his chief for several long seconds before replying.

'Well, in that case I'll finish cleaning off the drainage trolleys inside, sterilize some equipment and put the victim into the freezer, then I'll go home and see you first thing in the morning.'

'OK, thank you, Maxwell. I have to type some initial findings and observations before I go home. You finish off and get some rest.'

'You too, Doctor,' he replied, then walked away.

As he turned out of sight, Dr Laos found herself wishing that Maxwell would sometimes call her Karen, but this had never happened in the three years they had worked together.

Something told Karen Laos that she was going to find rest elusive. Her preliminary findings on the new victim were too familiar for her to articulate. With a heavy sigh, Dr Laos knew that something from her past, something terrible, had returned. The thought of seeing Detective Inspector Roberts the next day both invigorated and terrified her, for reasons of which she was not yet fully aware. *My preliminary findings.* She hadn't shared fully with her assistant the extent of her suspicions that had arisen from her first observations, as she herself was unsure of their significance.

She knew, however, that she was acting now not just with scientific method but by instinct. Maxwell had not been with her at the time of the first case she had been engaged in with Detective Inspector Roberts and for that reason there were aspects of her early findings that she had not been prepared to disclose to him during today's events. Ordinarily, Dr Laos was more than willing to have Maxwell at her side in all aspects of her work. Today, however, he had noticed that she preferred to work alone, only calling upon him for basic mortuary-assistant duties.

Saturday 8 October, 8.50 p.m.

He sat with his back against the oak-framed door of his late parents' wardrobe, concentrating on the feel and texture of the wood pressing into the small of his back. From this position he could see the full length of the sweeping gothic staircase that led down from the landing outside his bedroom to the main house. The rain lashed against the windowpane that ran along the wall to the right of where he sat and the wind was howling around the large, empty house, echoing through the decrepit windows and rotting wooden doors.

He preferred to keep minimal lighting, and often found

himself watching the shadows of the tall, downy birch trees flickering along the walls and floors of the vast expanse of his house, the house he had claimed upon his parents' death. *His mother had liked downy birch.* Her decomposing corpse, home-buried, had lain beneath those trees for eighteen years, since he was sixteen years old. Despite his physical stillness this evening, he had been more active in recent days. His six-year period of inactivity had been, like previous punctuations in time, a pause during which he felt himself growing in power, harnessing the energy he craved and fed from, settling down, hibernating and later feeding once more. Only now, things were different. He found his appetite for feeding increasing; his skill in his craft and the growing desires that it satisfied made him feel strong.

This was a man whose outlook on the world was like no other's. He was alone for much of his life, preferring existence to be this way. Solitary. Isolated. The ease with which he conducted himself when needed contrasted with his current psychological state. Deep within he felt a new urgency developing with regard to his work: the violence of which he was capable, the terror he inflicted and the strength he gained were all too real.

He had been created from the remnants of a life unattached to the outside world; the product of a complicated and dark set of circumstances. These circumstances would take Detective Inspector Roberts and Dr Laos to some of the darkest places they were ever to see in their careers, and would test their joint resolve and understanding beyond anything they could have expected.

As the wind picked up and the rain continued belting down at the windows of his large, desolate house, finding any crack to force itself into, he stood up slowly from his seated position. His physique was strong and muscular. He was wearing just his underpants and, holding his hands high above him into an arched shape, he shouted loud and deep the name 'Abeona'.

Chapter Two

Saturday 8 October, 9.05 p.m.,
Greater Manchester

Detective Inspector James Roberts paused momentarily as he pulled his car into a petrol station halfway between the M62 and M60 motorway interchanges. He was driving back to Manchester from Whitby; he had been unexpectedly called away on business in the early hours of the morning.

His frustration had grown throughout the day, as had his weariness and sense of fatigue. The case in Whitby had turned out to be a complete waste of his time and resources and he had clocked up close to 280 miles of driving in one day alone, several hours of travel and all for no good reason. He wanted to get back to the Manchester case as soon as possible. He was also finding the urge to climb into bed for some much-needed shut-eye before tomorrow morning's debrief difficult to ignore.

His sleep had been interrupted the previous night with the discovery of the body of a young male victim, found in the undergrowth of Saline Park in Manchester's eastern suburbs.

Roberts wanted this case and had intended to start his

preliminary work as soon as he had received the call from his detective chief inspector at 1 a.m. The body had been found by some late-night revellers making their way home to their student digs. Roberts' chief also knew that this was a case for the detective inspector and Roberts had been pleased to hear that it would be Dr Karen Laos who would lead up the pathology team at the city's mortuary.

Karen Laos, he thought to himself. That was a name he hadn't heard for a long time. He remembered her from an earlier case they had worked on together; remembered her professionalism and dedication. Calling her at three that morning would normally have been standard procedure, except that it was six years since Detective Inspector Roberts had worked on a child murder of this apparent nature in Manchester. He was desperate to hear more details and angry, too, that his first day on the case had been wasted. He needed to speak to Dr Laos. He also needed to speak to his colleagues to find out what the hell was going on.

Now, as he filled his car with some much-needed petrol, he pushed away from his mind the words 'not a normal murder'. At sixty years of age James Roberts was close to retirement, and twenty years of working in child homicide had failed to make him impervious to the differences between run-of-the-mill homicide and *this* type of crime. *That's a good thing,* he thought to himself. *It means I'm not an insensitive old dinosaur.*

The chilly night-time October air hurried him to complete his petrol transaction and get back into his car. He rubbed his hands for warmth before pulling away into a slip road where he ate half a cheese and tomato sandwich and a rapidly cooling coffee before setting off again. The rain had started again. The moors had been dark on his journey across and the rain had been on and off all day. Visibility had been poor, as it always was at this time of the year in this part of the country.

I'm sure the last time I saw Karen Laos was at this time of year, Roberts thought to himself. The circumstances were too similar for him to ignore, which was why he had wanted to get back to Manchester as soon as possible. He checked his watch and saw the time approaching 9.40 in the evening. Just as he had resigned himself to the fact that he would have to wait until the following morning, his mobile phone lit up and vibrated itself across his dashboard.

He reached his right hand up to his ear and enabled the Bluetooth device that meant he could speak safely and continue to drive. He waited as the device paired with the phone on the car's dashboard. He stole a quick look at the name flashing across the display: *Philip Morti.* Roberts' detective chief inspector. Flicking his mobile open, he took the call.

'Yes, Chief, how can I help you?' he answered.

'Good evening, James, are you back in Manchester yet?' There was a tone of urgency in his superior's voice.

'I'm about a half-hour out, give or take ten minutes for this nasty weather.'

Roberts threw a glance out of his window to mentally check his words with the conditions outside. He guessed he was about right.

'OK, well, I want you in the station as soon as you're back in town. And I want to make arrangements for Dr Laos to join you over here as well.'

Roberts paused a brief moment before responding, aware that his boss sounded slightly perplexed.

'But, sir, I don't think Dr Laos will be working at this time of night, plus I haven't heard anything all day from Anneka.'

Anneka Carlson was his partner; had been for the last

two years. She had a degree in psychology and had joined the force to pursue her special interest in violent crime when she was twenty-two; a little over a year after she had graduated. Detective Inspector Roberts liked her. He thought she was a little bit headstrong and naïve, but then hadn't he been the same when he was her age?

Now thirty-two years old, Anneka Carlson had worked her way quickly into the criminal investigation unit, having served three years as a uniformed officer before gaining her commission as a trainee detective constable at twenty-six. By the time Anneka Carlson had turned twenty-eight, she had completed the required national initial crime investigator's development programme and had made the rank of detective constable quicker than anyone James Roberts could recall over many years. Her determination had seemed unstoppable.

He only had her part-time as she was paid seventy-five per cent by homicide *proper* (there were not enough resources to spare her full-time to James Roberts and his speciality). The remaining twenty-five per cent of her salary came from local government funding. That had been a boost to Roberts' pride: someone high up valued his work and as a result he had Carlson working alongside him, although, if he were being honest with himself, not as much as he would have liked. His job was often lonely.

He had left her overseeing the case as he headed off to Whitby that morning and had expected to hear something from her by now.

'Anneka has been reporting to me today, James,' shot back Morti, with what Detective Inspector Roberts thought sounded like a satisfied and slightly condescending tone to his voice. 'As you were out of the area all day, I took over this one.'

Roberts wanted to reply that it had been Morti himself who had sent him on the wild-goose chase on which he had wasted his time, but he kept his composure.

'Well, that's fine, sir. What have we learnt so far?'

'Not much, James,' replied Morti. 'The pathologist hasn't given much away. She has the body in the mortuary and insists that she needs to speak to you.' He paused then finished his sentence. 'Before tomorrow morning.'

So Dr Laos *was* at work still and something told the detective inspector that his suspicions were about to be confirmed. This was a murder that would bring him and Dr Laos full circle, back to where they last parted ways six years ago. He snapped himself out of thought.

'In that case I will be with you as soon as possible.'

'Good,' replied Morti. 'And stop by the mortuary and collect the good doctor, will you? I'll get Anneka to call her now to tell her to expect you. The sooner we get a handle on what's going on here, the better for all of us. The press are already asking questions and we need a firm ID on the victim before we take any further steps.'

Another decision made for Roberts, Morti continued: 'I have had officers over at the mortuary all day and certain materials have been removed by SOCO.'

Certain materials? The words stayed a long moment in Detective Inspector Roberts' mind but he decided not to probe any further; he knew that he was needed back at his office, and the sooner the better. He ended the call and turned back onto the motorway, heading for Manchester's inner-city suburbs. If he were able to maintain sixty miles an hour he should find himself back in town within forty minutes.

Chapter Three

Saturday 8 October, 10.20 p.m.,
Central Manchester Mortuary

Dr Laos leaned the small of her back heavily into the chair as she sat at her desk. The mortuary was now empty, except for her and night security. Nothing much had changed here; the security guard, Roger, had been on the night shift for longer than the doctor could recall. A small desk lamp supplied enough light for her to work at her computer. Her office hadn't changed since the day she first took over the position more than a decade ago. It had a small four-by-eight rectangular top, giving her just enough room to keep her files in order. The walls were old and worn, made of simple timber partitions, which meant that on busy days she could hear the phones and voices from the corridors and offices close to her.

She had a direct view into the mortuary if she looked up though she rarely felt the need to do so these days. She trusted her colleagues and had learned to keep her personal office space separate from her work space. The mortuary itself was dark at this time of night with just some panel floor lighting in case of emergencies.

Dr Laos found herself tapping on the side of her desk with the pen in her left hand as she studied the computer screen in front of her. She had gone from being tired to exhausted and back to wakefulness all in a few hours. She read to herself her report summarizing her initial findings on the young victim whose body lay on a slab in her mortuary, knowing that she would shortly have to present these to the homicide detectives, among them being Detective Inspector James Roberts.

While she was reviewing her preliminary findings, her mobile phone rang. She clicked on the print icon as she answered it.

'Dr Laos. Good evening.'

It was a female voice she recognized from earlier in the afternoon.

'This is Detective Constable Anneka Carlson; we spoke earlier today.'

'Yes, Detective Constable, good evening. I've been expecting your call.'

The laser-jet printer started up as she spoke, spilling out three pages of A4 paper.

'I apologize for the delay in getting back to you,' Carlson said. 'My detective sergeant has informed me that you left a message asking to see us this evening rather than tomorrow morning.'

Dr Laos breathed an affirmative reply, adding, 'Have you been able to find Detective Inspector Roberts yet?'

'Yes, we have, which is why I'm calling you. The inspector is on his way back into the city now. He's going to call in at the mortuary to pick you up and bring you here to the station for a meeting. May I ask what you have found that you think we need to discuss this evening?'

The curiosity in the young detective constable's voice was apparent. Dr Laos decided to hold her ground until she met the officers in person.

'Actually, Detective Constable Carlson, I really would rather wait to reveal my initial findings until I am there.' After a momentary pause she continued: 'It's just that there are aspects of this case that are very similar to a previous case I worked on with Inspector Roberts and I really feel that he should be the first to hear about my findings . . . out of courtesy.'

Before Detective Constable Carlson had the chance to confirm that she understood, Dr Laos had to cut the call short as she saw Roger, the night security guard, approaching her office door. Behind him came the figure of a man she had not seen in a long while.

'Constable, I have to go. I have a feeling that your partner is on his way in. I look forward to meeting you shortly.'

Roger knocked on her office door, clearly curious as to why a senior police officer was visiting so late and, indeed, why Dr Laos was still in the building.

'Dr Laos,' Roger said, 'I have a visitor for you. This is Detective Inspector Roberts; he says that he has a meeting scheduled with you.'

Dr Laos stood up to greet her guest.

'Yes. Thank you for bringing Mr Roberts down to my office, although you could have called from the front desk and I would have come out.'

Before Roger had the chance to reply, Detective Inspector Roberts had entered the room, indicating that Roger should leave as he did so. Dr Laos found herself feeling guilty at having been unable at first to recall his name. How could she have forgotten this man? He was the same kind-faced, tired-looking policeman she had met six years previously when working on case AA-262, *the wounded child*, the memory of whom she had tried to suppress. Aspects of those memories came flooding back to her now as she found herself looking at Detective Inspector Roberts. It wasn't just the memory of the victim that she had tried to suppress but her memory of James Roberts too.

He wore a strikingly similar dark green tweed jacket and worn faded trousers that she recalled thinking had looked far too old and in need of replacing the last time she had seen him. She noted how his reading glasses hung around his neck on a brown string that looked as though it were home-made, and hanging from his pocket was a bunch of tissues, of which Roberts himself seemed totally unaware. His smile was still kindly and his features still attractive, if somewhat older looking.

Before Dr Laos had the chance to speak, Detective Inspector Roberts had taken her hand in his and was shaking it.

'Dr Laos, how nice it is to see you again,' he said, adding as an aside, 'although in our line of work we do seem to meet only over dead bodies and mortuary tables, don't we?'

Dr Laos was sure she caught a glint of something in his eye but could not place it. A fleeting thought ran through her mind: *maybe that's his put-me-at-ease line.* It worked.

'Detective Inspector, it's good to see you again as well, but we really should make a move.'

As Karen Laos spoke, she pulled her hand from his, put her paperwork into an envelope and picked up her bag. Detective Inspector Roberts recognized the professionalism that he had witnessed the last time the two had met but he also recalled that same feeling of being shut out by her. That was what he hadn't been able to place earlier. She liked to read other people's expressions but clearly did not like being scrutinized herself. Memories came flooding back to him.

'After you, Dr Laos,' he said, bowing in a manner that confused her and leaving her unsure as to whether he was being sarcastic or polite.

A few moments later she had signed herself out of the building at Roger's desk, and the two were in Detective Inspector Roberts' car en route to the police station.

Chapter Four

Sunday 9 October, 12.15 a.m.,
Greater Manchester Police Headquarters

Karen Laos had been in Manchester's main police station on several occasions in her capacity as a government pathologist but this was the first time she had been in Detective Chief Inspector Morti's office, although she had met him in the past. The journey to the station, usually fifteen minutes, had taken longer than expected because of the heavy night-time traffic and terrible weather conditions. The city itself looked tired and worn out. As far as Karen could recall it was the first time in her adult life she had sat in a passenger seat, staring out of a car window. Ordinarily she drove herself everywhere.

Part of her wondered why she had been collected in such a manner by Detective Inspector Roberts but she was grateful for the lift as she hadn't slept for almost twenty-four hours. She had a lot on her mind and Roberts had noted the way in which she clung on to the A4 envelope, which held her preliminary autopsy findings. She seemed distracted and he noticed her bite down on her lower lip, a subconscious movement that, he assumed, was designed to alleviate tension. He had tried to strike up a conversation, curious to know more about this woman as a person and as a professional. Something about her roused his interest but she didn't seem keen to give anything away.

The only subject on which she had replied with more than a grunt or a nod of her head was when he asked her whether she recalled the first time they had met. Her response had been heartfelt and animated, something he hadn't expected given her hitherto distant manner. She had turned her glance from the rain-sheeted window out of which she had been staring and addressed Roberts directly.

'Detective Inspector, the first time we met to work together on a case together was six years ago and it remains the only case that I have never managed to solve.'

James Roberts didn't know how to feel about this statement. *Was it an aspersion on his ability to detect and solve cases?* He had the feeling, though, that it was something more, something closely related to Dr Laos's own sense of failure on the case.

She clarified this in part when she continued by saying, 'To be quite honest with you, Inspector Roberts, when I received your call this morning at 3 a.m., I was quite shaken up. You . . . you have a reputation, shall we say, for only getting involved in cases that are quite . . . well, disturbing.'

'Disturbing?' he asked in response. 'And that's coming from a pathologist! You spend your working day with dead bodies and my line of work disturbs you?'

He had watched as she digested his question, thinking how best to answer.

'Inspector, I didn't mean that as an affront to you, but the fact that *you* called me and the fact that you are the only specialist in our entire region who works in child homicide told me immediately that this would be a day very much like the first day the two of us met one another on our last case.'

He had liked her answer and allowed her to continue talking.

'That is to say, I knew that the body that came to the mortuary this morning was going to be that of a child, and I also suspected severe trauma and sexual wrongdoing.'

Detective Inspector James Roberts had interrupted her at this point.

'Dr Laos, not all murderers get away with their crimes; just because we got unlucky last time doesn't mean that we are about to repeat the same pattern.'

As she sat now in Detective Chief Inspector Morti's office, those words and that conversation echoed around Karen's head.

She was hopeful that Roberts was correct but she knew something that he didn't: she knew the details contained in her initial findings, which she would very soon have to share with those who were about to assemble around her.

So far, only she and Detective Inspector Roberts had arrived; Philip Morti and Detective Constable Anneka Carlson were on their way. Dr Laos stared down at the plastic coffee cup in her hand, and a fleeting recollection came to mind. It had been only six hours since she had drunk the coffee from the faulty machine in her own office but it felt like days ago. She briefly thought of Maxwell and hoped he was sleeping. She would see him again in less than eight hours. She was woken from her deeply contemplative state when Detective Chief Inspector Morti and Detective Constable Carlson, Roberts' partner, came in through the door.

Detective Constable Carlson was striking in appearance. She greeted her partner with a hug and this, for some reason, took Karen Laos aback. She guessed that the tall, blonde detective was a good ten years younger than herself, and what a difference those ten years made. The constable's face was youthful and her smile instantly infectious. Karen did not feel in the mood for smiling, however, although she acknowledged it with a kind grin and said how pleased she was to meet her.

Philip Morti was just as Dr Laos remembered him: a bald, fat man of no more than five foot four inches tall who seemed to sweat profusely. He had a small voice but barked when he felt the need. He was full of energy this evening and pink around the cheeks. He was quick to usher his guests around his large mahogany desk and get the discussion under way.

As he sat down in his bulky leather seat, he appeared even smaller than on first impressions. He somehow sank, seemingly half swallowed, into his chair, his puffy face peeking out over the desk. Karen had been sandwiched between Detective Inspector Roberts and Detective Constable Carlson, with far less room to herself than she was accustomed to. When invited by Morti to divulge her findings so far, she took the opportunity to give herself some space by standing up, a movement that grabbed the attention of all in the room. She was taller than he'd remembered, and Roberts couldn't help but find her quite beautiful.

Behind her thoughtful eyes lurked a beauty which Roberts felt had been kept on a leash on purpose. Her short, dark-brown neck-length haircut was now fully revealed and Roberts contemplated how the first time he had seen her she had had her hair tucked beneath a tight-fitting hat, for they had been in the mortuary. They had spent the majority of their time together back then in the mortuary, as Karen's status then was only junior pathologist.

'Detective Chief Inspector, colleagues, I won't pretend that today has been easy,' she started, offering a semi-smile to her audience. 'I have done some preliminary work on the victim, whose identity remains unknown, and I will run through the details that I have at this early stage. I will also offer to you some early suspicions that have crossed my mind.'

Morti shot her a look.

'What do you mean by "suspicions", Dr Laos?'

'All will become clear during the course of my review of my observations,' Dr Laos told him curtly.

Dr Laos caught a smirk from Roberts aimed at Anneka Carlson; clearly they liked to see their chief being put in his place. Morti grew redder in the cheeks but said nothing.

'My external examinations reveal that our victim, classified for now as case AD-482, appears to be that of a male of approximately eleven years old. I confirm that the deceased arrived by ambulance escorted by police into the Central Manchester Mortuary at 4.30 on the morning of Saturday 8 October. The victim was found in Saline Park, approximately thirty metres off the main pedestrian track.

'Forensic scientists from my team and the police have secured the area. As of this time, they have not been able to identify the way in which the body was delivered to the park. There are no clear signs of vehicle tracks and there are several footprints in the soil, possibly belonging to the group that found the body. We will be able to eliminate any other footprints that do not belong to the group, given time. The heavy rain is likely to have washed any defining evidence away. The deceased arrived in a body bag and had no identifiable clothing or belongings.'

Detective Inspector Roberts' face looked sombre.

'The victim was found by members of the public in a local park. It was buried beneath greenery. The body shows severe signs of trauma. The pupils of the eyes were dilated. Trauma appears to be consistent with prolonged malnutrition and ante-mortem physical injury of a sexual nature. Anal trauma as a result of a crude surgical procedure is apparent.'

Dr Laos took a breath and clarified her words.

'I use the term "sexual" only to describe the area of the victim's body where the perpetrator of this crime concentrated his efforts. I do not mean that the victim was sexually assaulted; at least not in the sense of rape or molestation.'

She saw the confused expression on the faces of her colleagues and went into further detail.

'It appears that the victim's rectum was disturbed by the perpetrator, but not to satisfy sexual desire. The markings of the injury would appear to be more ritualistic, more needs-driven in that the killer was attempting to satisfy a different type of desire from that of a sexual nature. I have detected traces of hydrogen peroxide around the victim's anus and there are superficial cut wounds, as if a surface layer of the victim's skin has been removed.'

Detective Inspector Roberts stood up with an alarmed look on his face.

'Dr Laos, is this leading us to where I think it might be?'

Dr Laos looked back at him. 'Unfortunately, yes, Inspector. I think we may be looking at the same criminal we encountered but never identified six years ago.'

'Six years?' interrupted Morti, his voice becoming higher with each word. 'Are you suggesting, Doctor, that we have a pattern repeating, that the unidentified murderer from six years ago may still be active?'

'If, Mr Morti, you are asking whether we have a serial killer on our hands, I cannot give you a conclusive answer. If, however, you are asking whether this is the same killer, I think that when you have heard what I am about to tell you, you will have to agree that yes, it is.'

The faces in the room grew ashen, but nobody spoke except Dr Laos.

'The removal of the victim's skin is common in cases of so-called trophy killers. A psychologist specializing in this area can better enlighten you in this regard but the use of hydrogen peroxide and superficial skin removal was seen also in case AA-262.'

Detective Inspector James Roberts nodded his head in agreement for the benefit of the others in the room, a movement that told them that he recalled the case well.

'Dr Laos, if you can, cast your mind back six years. I believe that at that time we had a conversation about the gender of the perpetrator of the crime. I only mention this because of the details you have provided us with so far. Am I right to say that the ritualistic and violent nature of this case is more likely to be associated with a male perpetrator rather than a female?'

Dr Laos carefully considered her response.

'Without making sweeping generalizations, yes. Research has shown us many times that men, overall, are more likely to commit all types of crimes. There is some evidence that derives from the study of hormones and how male and female brains process information. The use of PET scans, which use radiation in order to produce three-dimensional images of various organs in the body, have shown that male brains, as opposed to female brains, produce a higher level of specific hormones in specific brain areas.

'You might be surprised to learn that murderers do not have higher levels of testosterone than people that do not commit murder. However, the evolutionary theory of criminology suggests that in our ancestral past, males were more actively involved in hunting. As a result of this it is fair to say that the type of controlled aggressiveness it would take to commit the kind of murder we are discussing now would almost certainly derive from a male killer.'

Dr Laos looked at the faces of her colleagues. She noted that they were processing the information she had given them.

'Women that commit murder tend not to use violent methods. Poisoning, for example, is largely a female crime, whereas a male that kills more than once is likely to be motivated sexually. These categories of male killers are also far more elusive, far rarer and have little or no empathy.'

Dr Laos felt that she had provided a sufficient response to Detective Inspector Roberts' question about the gender of the killer and decided to continue with what she had been saying about hydrogen peroxide.

'Hydrogen peroxide has several uses,' she continued. 'Primarily, in low strengths, it is a very effective cleaning material and will have minimal negative effect on human skin. However, in higher concentrations, formula at, say, over thirty-five per cent H_2O_2 strength it can be used to clean tougher materials, such as bones. If exposed to human skin it would cause the type of mucous membrane blistering and discolouration that I have detected in our current victim's rectal area, and that which we found in the case of AA-262, six years ago.'

Morti made a note in his pad. *Check sellers of*

industrial-strength hydrogen peroxide.

Roberts, all too aware of the connections, added aloud for the sake of all present, 'In our last investigation the hydrogen peroxide found on the victim could not be traced to any seller at the time; it was found to be old and no longer on the market.'

Morti added a question mark to his note.

Dr Laos continued.

'Manual strangulation marks are also evident around the deceased's neck. The strangulation indents were probably inflicted around midday on Friday. That is, at least, my impression on examination. Toxicology results will confirm suspicions that the victim was drugged and therefore incapacitated in the hours and days leading to death. Blood-work was sent for analysis early Saturday morning and is expected back within twenty-four hours.'

Detective Constable Carlson asked her first question of the meeting so far.

'What makes you think the victim had been drugged prior to being murdered?'

Detective Inspector Roberts interjected.

'Anneka, this case seems to have all the hallmarks of the previous unsolved case that Dr Laos spoke of. If we are indeed dealing with the same killer, our latest victim will probably have been drugged with benzodiazepines prior to death, which would have caused significant drowsiness and cognitive impairment.'

Karen Laos, not sure whether everyone in the room was fully aware of the importance in such cases of benzodiazepines, decided to offer a brief explanation of their uses.

'Benzodiazepines are an important class of drugs with a broad range of therapeutic effects, including sedative-hypnotic, anxiolytic, muscle-relaxant and anti-convulsant. Because they are widely used there is a risk of benzodiazepines interacting with other central nervous system depressants, which can make it dangerous for the subject to drive a car. Benzodiazepines are now among the most commonly prescribed drugs; this increases the likelihood of addiction and abuse, and often they are found in combination with other drugs in drug-related fatalities or drug-facilitated sexual assault cases.'

She had used the words 'sexual assault cases' to ensure that her colleagues in the room would understand the point that she was making. Morti and Carlson were making notes so she felt sure she had piqued their interest.

She paused and studied the facial expressions of the others in the room before continuing.

'Here comes the crucial evidence. The body of the deceased had been dressed in a grey towelling gown with the word "Abeona" stitched in red into the weave of the fabric. I and I believe you too have seen this only once in the past: that is in our case that remains unsolved.'

'What is "Abeona"?' Carlson asked.

Detective Inspector Roberts provided the answer.

'The term "Abeona" was found in our last case to refer directly to a mythological goddess from the ancient Roman religion, said to protect children from the time they left their parents' home, thus safeguarding the first steps that they took alone. This deity was among the *di indigetes* – indigenous gods – of Rome, abstract deities and concepts that predated the many later syncretisms of various cultures' mythologies.'

'You sound like a walking library, Inspector,' said Morti. Having looked more than slightly pleased with himself,

Detective Inspector Roberts' face grew more serious as he answered his superior.

'This is not a case I have ever forgotten,' he replied.

Dr Laos semi-smiled at him; the two shared a unique understanding with regard to the complexity of the case. *Nor could you ever forget it.*

Morti noted the silence that prevailed in the room as everyone digested the information they had heard. He stood up, looking at the faces of his colleagues and Dr Laos, and took his chance to address the meeting, this time his voice more steady and less shrill.

'Thank you, Dr Laos, for your overview. From the policing angle we have much work to do. To this end, I would like to ask you to work closely with Detective Inspector Roberts on this case, as the two of you share a common experience which seems to be related to the present case.'

Work closely with Roberts. The detective chief inspector's request seemed more like a command as Karen let the words sink in but she could do little other than concur with the last words he had spoken. He was right about the two of them sharing a common experience. She had half expected that this suggestion would be made.

Sitting close to Morti's desk, deep in thought, Detective Constable Anneka Carlson looked somewhat left out of the conversation. She straightened her comportment when she realized that everyone else was looking at her. She asked the question that Roberts had felt sure would follow.

'Sir, if I may ask, what will be my angle in this investigation if Detective Inspector Roberts will be working with Dr Laos?'

'Constable,' replied Morti, 'there is plenty of work to go round for everyone in this room; I need you to work with the incident room and the officers who attended the crime scene late Friday night. You will need to follow up on identifying the victim. I want you to check missing person reports, liaise with other constabularies. Speak to whoever you need to. Pair up with Detective Constable Buzan in forensics; he is already aware of the case.'

He paused, thinking, *Half the damn city will be soon*, before continuing, 'Dr Laos's team has submitted the physical evidence to the scientists working in his division. I want you to liaise with them where appropriate; follow up any leads that present themselves. I want details on that fabric our victim was wrapped in; dig out the previous case, find any similarities in material, look at manufacturers, push for prints, go and visit the goddamn witnesses who found the body.'

He had said a lot, none of it irrelevant, and Karen Laos respected the manner in which he had succinctly delivered his commands. She saw that he was clearly affected by this case and felt a growing respect for his professionalism.

'Dr Laos,' started Detective Inspector Roberts as he looked at his watch, half mouthing the words 'half-past one in the morning', 'as it's late, is there anything else you need to add before we close this meeting? It is important that we all get some rest before we reconvene in the morning.'

Dr Laos knew he was right; the energy surge that she had felt earlier now seemed to be ebbing away into the hours of the night. She collected her thoughts quickly, studied her computer-printed notes and concluded her preliminary findings.

'The body has multiple small areas of haemorrhage bilaterally in the conjunctiva. Asphyxiation by manual strangulation is evident, with pinpoint haemorrhages in the skin, suggesting that the victim was not strangled by ligature but by hand. I would hazard a guess that strangulation will be found to have been the primary cause of death, with other evidence accounting for secondary and possibly tertiary causes. This is also consistent with the previous mentioned case: AA-262.'

She paused to ensure that she had everybody's full attention. She did.

'There is no evidence of a struggle between the victim and the assailant, which further suggests that the victim was pharmaceutically incapacitated. Had a struggle taken place it is likely that fingernail marks would have been observed. No such physical scarring is present. I have also identified what appear to be recent signs of injury along the victim's inner arm. Physical examination suggests that these pinprick-size indentations are the result of an intravenous injection.'

Detective Inspector Roberts grew lively as she spoke.

'But this is not something that I recall from our last victim.'

His statement was loaded with both query and fact.

'You are correct, Inspector, no such signs of intravenous injection were ever found in the last victim, which makes it important that we obtain the full blood-test results in the morning. Any foreign substance that may be detected, that had not been metabolized by the victim's body or, indeed, had dissipated by itself prior to death, will certainly show up.'

'So,' interjected Morti, 'why would the killer have changed his technique this time around?'

'A reasonable guess would be that the perpetrator has developed more of a refined taste for his murders and is perfecting his technique to enhance the effect of the ritual that he enacts,' said Dr Laos.

Her audience looked impressed.

'Or,' offered Roberts, 'the killer is feeling lonely and has started the process of interacting with the outside world. This is not uncommon when repeat offenders start to feel smug or seek attention; they often up the ante, not realizing that their change of tactics would be likely to help us catch them.'

'Unless,' said Dr Laos, 'he wants to be caught.'

The room was quiet for thirty seconds.

'That is also a possibility if the killer has started to unconsciously feel worthless,' agreed Roberts. 'Either way, I suspect that this change in tactic will ultimately help us in our investigations.'

He certainly hoped this would be the case.

As her finger moved along the A4 paper from which she read, Dr Laos felt her hand twitching, probably from tiredness.

'I have conducted some preliminary internal examinations, based upon a hunch from previous experience with case AA-262, and found that upon examination of the victim's throat, the palatine tonsils have been removed.'

Detective Inspector Roberts' interest and disgust were evident in his facial expression as he raised his hand to his face and massaged the area around his eyes.

'The nature and pattern of injury and scarring suggests that the tonsils have been removed post death.' *Which is some small comfort*, she added in her own head. 'The amateurish manner in which the removal has been made is consistent with case AA-262. The right and left pleural cavity contains ten millilitres of clear fluid with no adhesions. The pericardial sac is yellow, glistening without adhesions or fibrosis and contains thirty millilitres of a straw-coloured fluid. There is minimal fluid in the peritoneal cavity.'

'Dr Laos,' intervened Morti, 'I will ask archives to deliver to all of us a copy of the last case, as we may find leads and clues that we missed last time.'

He noticed Detective Inspector Roberts' face falling and quickly added, 'Not because the last investigation was conducted poorly but because we now have two victims, seemingly murdered by the same individual and the similarities in both cases are overwhelming. We also have far better forensic facilities at our disposal than we did at the time of the first murder. Maybe we can identify the tools that the killer would have needed to extract the victim's tonsils. We are looking at both similarities and differences in the case of AA-262. You all know what you have to do. Let's make sure we catch the person responsible this time.'

He looked directly at Roberts, who was deep in thought, before adding, 'And you, Inspector Roberts, I would like you to speak to one of the forensic psychologists and devise an updated profile of the killer. I know you're good at doing that alone but we need to cross the Is and dot the Ts very carefully to ensure that we are all following a clear map from the start.'

It was all that Roberts could do to nod his approval of his senior's idea. *I will do that with my new partner, Dr Laos,* he thought, slightly curious as to why she hadn't objected to being recruited temporarily by the police force.

Karen Laos had given some thought to this very issue but had concluded that she wasn't the only pathologist working at the Central Manchester Mortuary; she had plenty of excellent colleagues who could take other cases. She would, however, need to speak briefly to her supervisor to inform him of her plans. Either way, she worked for the government and she would be tied to this case until a satisfactory conclusion was reached: she was the pathologist on duty when the case came in. *And the call from Roberts,* she found herself adding.

Chapter Five

Sunday 9 October, 5.30 a.m.

His sleep had been patchy as always. He liked this time of the year and this hour of the day. His house provided secrecy and privacy and he rarely had the need for human contact. No callers, no flyers through the door. A large six-bedroom pre-Victorian house set in ten acres of woodland, secluded. The house had once been visible from the village that had existed back in the 1960s and 1970s. That village had been demolished in the late 1980s, an area of green-belt land having sprung up in all directions from the house, making the expansive ten-acre grounds seem even larger.

He paid little attention to the crumbling shell of the house's exterior, and more to the detail internally. He had slept in the same bedroom since he was a child, and recalled his parents' demand for quietness; they had not liked to be disturbed by him or others. The five remaining bedrooms had not been touched since his parents had died.

As an only child, he had grown up home-schooled. At thirty-four years of age, he was alone in the world, but had over the years worked hard to become something else. He set his mind to the fact that his work would continue, as would his transformation. His mother had been fifty years old when she had conceived, his father ten years older. They had met a decade earlier, his mother having made the permanent move from Australia to the United Kingdom. Their marriage had started much like any other, until his father had decided to move the two into what his mother had termed 'the middle of nowhere'.

His father had been abusive, an alcoholic with a predisposition to using his fists. His alcohol dependence had grown upon the death of his own aging mother, who had spent the last two years of her life an invalid, wheelchair bound, or sitting in her favorite rocking chair in the greenhouse. She had moved in with her son and his Australian wife when their own son was just three years old.

His memories of his grandmother, who had died when he was just five, were shadowy and irregular. He had known no relatives other than his parents and his grandmother and had had very little human contact outside their small family circle. As a child he had watched his mother cowering in the corner of rooms, hiding from her loud, rampaging husband. He had heard him coming, like a hurricane, sweeping through the house and its passageways, seeking out his wife.

His mother had tried to protect him too, often hiding him in the cellar when her husband took to his bouts of fury. As a young child, there was very little that he could have done to help his mother. His father had calmed down somewhat when his mother was diagnosed with multiple sclerosis, her condition developing rapidly when she reached the age of fifty-seven. Rather than beat his wife, he had then taken his fury out on his son.

The inflammatory disease had damaged her brain and spinal cord, breaking down the communication between the neurons and cells, leaving her to suffer horrendous bouts of pain. Every cold or flu she developed made the condition that much worse, her own immune system fighting her body rather than her infections. His father had been adamant that no nurses would visit, no doctors would call. She had made do with paracetamol, mild non-steroidal anti-inflammatories and occasional benzodiazepines that she had been given by a concerned neighbour who lived on the outskirts of their ten-acre estate. By the time she had turned sixty-five, the disease had taken hold of her entire body and her husband, then almost seventy-six, had instructed his sixteen-year-old son to suffocate her whilst she slept.

He had refused, by that point being physically stronger than his father, but his father had insisted.

'It is because of you that your mother is in so much pain. If you had the guts to do the right thing, you would put her out of her misery,' he had told him. *'It was your birth that caused her sickness.'*

He had looked at his father, a pathetic waif of a man, a shadow of his former self, and had felt total disgust and anger. It was the one and only time in his life that he had felt real emotion. It would be the only emotion that he would feel in future years as his psychopathic personality grew stronger and replaced any remnants of the humanity he had been robbed of.

One evening early in October his father had ordered from his son his nightly whisky, less of a shot-sized glass and more of a half-pint. He made his way down into the cellar and headed in the direction of his father's home-made distilled alcohol, stored in several wooden casks of charred white oak. He reached for his father's favourite pint glass, a soda-lime drinking vessel that sat on a makeshift wooden shelf protruding from the stone walls of the cellar. He opened the tap situated halfway down one of the wooden casks and poured a little over 350 millilitres. As he poured he thought of his father's words; his instructions to put his mother out of her suffering.

It was in that moment that he decided to put both out of their suffering, in the process hoping to alleviate his own. He made his way back up into the kitchen, from where he could hear his father hollering from the sitting room.

'Where the hell is my goddamned drink, you slow-witted fool?'

He paused in the kitchen and searched for the benzodiazepines that he knew were stored in one of the two large refrigerators in front of him.

He had been surprised to see that there was not only one small glass bottle of them but an entire box containing more than twenty bottles, each with thirty tablets of two-milligram-strength clonazepam. Their kind neighbour had been generous. He emptied ten tablets from one of the small bottles onto the kitchen surface, twenty milligrams in total, reached for the pestle and mortar from underneath the wooden cupboard that stored grains and pulses, and began grinding the medication until it was nothing more than a white powder.

As he emptied the powder into his father's pint glass, he took a spoon and stirred the contents until there were no visible signs of the concealed medication within. He headed to the sitting room where his father sat, half-reclined in a red velvet cushioned chair. The rain fell heavy against the windows, darkened out by thick maroon-coloured drapes.

A gramophone sat on the floor playing 'Mr Turnkey' by Zager and Evans. The time was coming up close to eight in the evening. His father had already finished a bottle of red wine, which lay empty on the rug at the base of his chair. A half-smoked cigarette sat in an already overfilled ashtray on the table besides his father's chair.

'Son,' his father said as he noticed him approaching, 'you know how grateful I am for you.' His father was pissed, his mood labile and subject to change when incapacitated. His son did not reply. He passed him his whisky and walked away, the lyrics from 'Mr Turnkey' echoing in his head as he left.

'He's calling out to his jailor to let him know he nailed his hand to the cell wall and is dying.'

He walked upstairs to where his mother lay sleeping, edging slowly into the musky room, the shadows of the downy birch trees dancing across the walls. He lifted from the side of her bed a large red-weave cushion and, tears rolling from his eyes, held it over her face. She had struggled momentarily but quickly stopped. He had never cried before. He promised himself that he never would again. He left his mother's corpse lying in her bed for two long days before burying her remains. He had purposefully waited for her body to turn cold and flaccid, rigor mortis having passed.

As he made his way back downstairs, his father was already unconscious, the combination of a bottle of red wine, twenty milligrams of sedatives and just over half a pint of whisky having taken its toll. However, he wanted his father to feel pain, not to simply drift away in peace. He slapped him hard around the face several times until he saw the stirrings of consciousness coming through. His father barely had time to lift his frail arms as he reached out and placed his hands around his neck, squeezing hard and persistently until he saw the veins in his now wide open eyes start popping red blood.

He squeezed for a long while before throwing his now-dead father's body to the floor. With his corpse he did not wait as he had with his mother. He utilized the three hours he knew he would have before rigor mortis started to take hold to drag his father's warm and flaccid lifeless body down into the cellar. He thought it would be fitting for his father's final resting place to be inside one of the larger charred white oak casks of whisky. He threw the body inside and sealed it closed, his watery grave where he would decompose in the alcohol that he had spent so many years perfecting.

Sunday 9 October, 6 a.m.

He had, as now, spent much of his time in the grounds of the house where he had taught himself to catch animals. Not to eat, but simply to study, as he liked to study any living creature; *to become something other than that which was restrained within his human body.* This morning he recalled his first kill and turned his mind back in time to his formative years as a young boy. A stray cat he had found aged seven wandering in his garden. He looked at the world through distant eyes, and the cat had been simply another image in the world that he felt so disconnected from. His reality had been formed in his head and in the confines of his house.

It came easily enough; he had taught himself to be superficially connected to the external world and fooled the black-tan cat into thinking he had wanted to play. As he walked now to the cellar underneath his kitchen on the lower floor, he remembered wanting to feel the cat, not only from the outside, but from the inside too. He had wrapped his hands around its throat and watched its life ebb away; fuelling his desire to see what was on the inside. His excitement had grown and in those formative experiences he had felt his first sexual awakenings.

He had been afraid at first of his parents' reaction – *they could get mad with me, very mad* – so he had hidden the lifeless cat in the bushes of the garden before returning some weeks later with a knife he had stolen from his father's garage. Not just any knife but a Swedish gutting knife, very adaptable and extremely sharp, with a high-friction grip handle. The blade had been cold-rolled special stainless steel. With this he had cut through the dead cat's fur, removing it piece by piece. Then, like a scientist, he had studied every small detail of its colour, texture, smell and even taste.

He had ripped the carcass open and stuck his bare hands inside, feeling the dead animal's organs. He had to have what was inside for keeps. There was no way he was going to let go of his prize. He had watched his father many times catch animals for food but had no interest in eating this animal. All he wanted was to keep it as a trophy. Its bones especially; they had excited him as a young boy. His father had animal bones on display in the house but he wanted these for himself; to secretly adore and touch when he wanted, at his will. His parents had gone away for a night, as they often did, leaving him alone.

He didn't know where they had gone; they rarely let him know their plans or movements. The dead cat would keep him busy for hours. In the same kitchen he now paused in as he thought back in time; he had scrubbed the bones of the animal with hot water and his mother's dish soap, removing greasy residue. He couldn't reach the sink so had had to push an overturned bucket under the sink to stand on.

He spent a long time that night many years ago washing the bones, feeling excited and stimulated as he touched them. They had been his. His father had done this many times with deer and antelope remains to hang along the walls, so he knew where he stored the large plastic drums of hydrogen peroxide – in one of the garden outhouses, of which there were three.

He also knew that he would have to soak his new possessions in the peroxide for a minimum of three days if he wanted the white colour to really come through.

'Watch, boy, be strong like a man,' his father had told him. *'Higher peroxide concentrations will bleach faster than lower peroxide concentrations.'*

He had learnt by reading books that certain bone preservers preferred to retain some of the natural off-white colouration while others, like him, preferred totally whitened bones. He certainly didn't like the alternative method of painting concentrated peroxide directly onto the bone. There was no fun in that, no personal care or attention.

As he stood now looking down at the trapdoor that led to his cellar, he felt pride in the fact that he had become a man. He had worked hard to get his toned muscular physique. He had learned that he had to, from the time his father first beat him as punishment for his cat bones. He had thought that his father would be pleased. His father had beaten him until he was bruised and his backside bled from being trampled with the leather studded belt that he would see so often thereafter. But he had managed to keep the bones of his kill and now as he walked down the narrow stairway into his cellar, he could place their exact location in the vast room beneath the house, as he could with all of his trophies. His attention fixed, he made his way to his newest addition, a smile starting to form between the corner of his lips and the edge of his eyes.

Chapter Six

Sunday 9 October, 6.15 a.m.,
Salford Quays, Greater Manchester

Karen Laos had set her alarm for 6.30 a.m. despite not having reached her home until almost 2.30. She reasoned that four hours' sleep was adequate and even if it wasn't, it was all she would be able to allow herself. After leaving Greater Manchester Police Headquarters with Detective Inspector Roberts as her chauffeur, she had returned briefly to the mortuary and waved a tired acknowledgement to Roger before collecting her car and driving home. She had spoken only a few words to Detective Inspector Roberts whilst in his car. Both were exhausted.

She was pleased to reach her own home and, as she pulled her BMW Z4 into the underground parking lot of Grain Wharf, Salford Quays, where she had lived for the past eight years, Karen Laos dared to sense for the first time in twenty-four hours a feeling of relief. It was short lived, as she knew it would be, but all the same it had been a welcoming experience to take the lift to her penthouse flat.

Karen remembered the area before its radical renovation

in 1982. Her father had worked in shipping in the dockyards of the city when she was a child and she had grown up only a few miles away from where her new home in Grain Wharf stood. From the top floor she enjoyed uninterrupted views of Mariner's Canal, the best vantage point being her bedroom veranda. This was a cold city for much of the year, but in the summer months, when the rain came less often, Karen enjoyed what little time to herself she could obtain sitting on her veranda and reminding herself how lucky she had been. *Lucky.* Now, as she heard the sound of her alarm clock waking her from her sleep, she contemplated the meaning of the word. To look around her apartment as an outsider, one might wonder how lucky she really had been. Yes, it was apparent she had a good job, that she earned good money, but the striking feature of her home was its lack of personal effects.

Standard-issue flat-pack furniture, found in a thousand other residences in the city, made her apartment somewhat nameless. Bland even. Mass-produced artwork adorned the walls of both Karen's living room and bedroom, the type one could find at any furniture shop. Not unattractive; just impersonal. Any visitor to her apartment would find it hard to locate a single item that indicated her individuality.

There were no photographs of family, of graduation, no mementos of any kind, except an extensive bookshelf, which interestingly contained no works of fiction. All of her books were academic, related to pathology and forensic science. *I prefer it this way*, she had thought. As she continued to wake up to the sound of her alarm, the tiredness stinging the corners of her eyes, Karen realized that remaining safe was what mattered to her. She really couldn't abide the thought of being hurt again. *Not like before.*

As she stepped into her slippers and contemplated what

would undoubtedly be another long day ahead, she tried to shrug off the thought of her failed ex-relationship. She had been in love with Mark but he hadn't been able to be her rock, to support her in her academic studies. He had not been, as she had hoped, her *come what may*. Her work had proven itself more steady and reliable than any of her failed attempts at relationships.

Her mother's words came back to her with a painful yet familiar realization: *'Karen, you are never going to find a husband spending all your time with dead bodies.'* It wasn't that she wasn't close to her mother; they were just different, in more ways than one.

After her father's death she had thought that she might grow closer to her mother, even hoped so, but it had not been the case. She had one sibling, a brother who had moved to South Africa when he had completed his university studies. Like her he had pursued medicine yet unlike her he was a routine, *run-of-the-mill*, as she liked to tell herself, general practitioner.

She had little more than an hour to get herself together and be at the mortuary by eight o'clock. At least the traffic wouldn't be so heavy on a Sunday morning. Coffee would come first as she entered her compact and tidy kitchen. Her filter coffee machine was set to 6.15 a.m., timed around her working schedule, as was the rest of her life.

Sunday 9 October, 7.45 a.m., Greater Manchester Police Headquarters

Detective Constable Anneka Carlson had parked her car in the secure car park of the police station and was making her way through the rain to the back door of the building that led into CID. She often had to pinch herself when she saw the name emblazoned across the department's entrance, *Criminal Investigation Department.* It had been her dream for a long while to move away from the uniformed beat and break into CID. She had certainly done well, as many people had told her since she had started in the department.

Her sense of pride had been enhanced when she had been assigned to work with Detective Inspector Roberts, whose reputation in the station had been long established. He was known to many as an eccentric, slightly dishevelled and clumsy man, with his mismatched clothes and unorthodox manner of working, his long-past-its-best heap of a Vauxhall Cavalier, which he politely refused to change. *'If it ain't broken don't fix it.'* Anneka rolled her eyes in amused acceptance as she recalled the number of times she had heard her superior say those words to her.

She did however have a great admiration and respect for her superior, which she had quickly discovered was shared by the rest of the station, even by Detective Chief Inspector Morti.

'Roberts will look after you, Anneka,' he had told her. He had been right. Detective Inspector Roberts rarely got it wrong and Carlson had seen the expression in his eyes late last night when they had had their conference with Dr Karen Laos. She knew that the importance Roberts attached to the current case was of the highest level and she sensed his personal affront at having not been able to catch the killer the last time around.

He was a perfectionist when it came to his work and the fact that a case had been left unsolved left her nervy; she suspected that he would go to any lengths to resolve the situation. She had also seen the dynamics between Roberts and Dr Karen Laos and, although she hadn't fully understood the meaning, she knew that both shared a heavy burden of memory which, when coupled with the dedication the two showed to their respective professions, would surely create an explosive partnership, be it good or otherwise.

For these reasons alone, Anneka reasoned, she would do her utmost to play her part in solving this case. She had been studious in her note-taking during last night's conference. She had prepared a long list of things that she had to do and now, as she approached her desk in an already busy incident room, she prepared herself for the day ahead. She would start by calling her newly assigned partner on this case, Detective Constable Frank Buzan in forensics, and arrange to meet him.

He had been expecting her call.

'Yes, Detective Constable Carlson, I've been looking forward to hearing from you,' he said when he answered his phone. He seemed to have as much energy and enthusiasm as she herself. 'I have made some appointments for us to follow up on the witnesses that found the victim on Friday night.'

Carlson found herself slightly taken aback. That was going to be her job.

'Oh, well, thank you, Detective Constable Buzan. I had planned to make those calls this morning.'

He stopped her in her tracks.

'No need, Anneka. May I call you Anneka?'

For someone she had only met once or twice during conferences, she didn't quite know how to respond but found herself agreeing with him.

'Err, yes, I guess that's fine.'

He started again. 'And please call me Fuz.'

Anneka tried to hide her surprise, not to mention amusement, and asked, 'Fuz?'

'It's a long story, from my days in police training. Maybe I'll tell you about it one day,' he replied.

She supposed that maybe one day he might. 'OK.' She paused. 'Fuz. So, tell me about the appointments you've made for us.'

'Well, I made an early start, with the help of some of my uniformed colleagues, of course. On Friday night there were three people who found the victim, and uniform have been around to knock on their door this morning.'

Anneka, somewhat taken aback, replied, 'On a Sunday morning, you sent uniform around to bang on the door of a group of students?'

'Early bird catches the worm, Anneka,' he said. 'Besides, I had a hunch that they would not have been out partying last night, not after what happened to them on Friday night.'

Detective Constable Carlson found herself agreeing with her new partner's assessment.

'Did your *hunch* turn out to be correct?' she asked.

'Yes, I was right,' Fuz replied, somewhat smugly. 'It seems that our witnesses, well, the closest thing we have to witnesses, are a pretty level-headed group.'

'How so?' asked Detective Constable Carlson.

'Two guys, one girl. She is a third-year law student. The guys are both in their second year studying some artsy degrees.' He cleared his throat and continued. 'All three were pretty shaken up from Friday. I have the original reports they gave to the cops that answered the 999 call. I'll email them over to you now if you like.'

Anneka Carlson found herself feeling several paces behind her partner.

'Please do that. Although I doubt there will be much in the reports.'

Fuz concurred. 'Yep, just standard uniform crime-scene paperwork. That said, however, the two men and the young lady have agreed to see us today so I suggested that we go to their place around lunchtime. Does that suit you?'

Given that Fuz had taken the metaphorical ball and run with it, Carlson could do little but agree.

She replied as she opened the inbox on her computer screen. 'That suits me. In the meantime I see that the detective chief inspector has emailed a copy of the original case report from six years ago.'

'Oh,' responded Fuz. 'I don't seem to have received a copy.'

Anneka finally felt that she had the upper hand.

'I will send you a copy over now.'

She clicked on the forward icon and sent a copy to Buzan.

As she read the email on the screen, she saw that Dr Karen Laos and Detective Inspector Roberts had been copied in on it, along with someone by the name of Trevor Stephenson. She clicked on her global address book and found him listed as a forensic psychologist. *The chief inspector certainly isn't wasting any time here*, she thought.

'The chief told me that the team working with Dr Laos had sent your scientists the physical evidence collected at the crime scene,' Anneka said, her tone less of a question and more of a statement.

'That's right,' Fuz replied. 'I have seen the handiwork for myself, just briefly. The son of a bitch makes his own handmade towelled gowns.'

'How do you know the killer is a male?' asked Anneka, curious as to what Detective Constable Buzan's response would be.

'Another hunch,' replied Fuz. 'They usually are in these cases.'

Detective Constable Carlson agreed.

'That's something we discussed in last night's conference. Dr Laos and Detective Inspector Roberts both feel confident that the killer is male.'

Fuz filled the short silence that followed.

'It's still early days before the science guys can tell us a great deal about the origins of the fabric but . . .'

He paused.

'What is it?' Anneka asked.

'The email you just sent me, look at page seven.' Detective Constable Carlson opened the attachment she had just sent and scanned down as instructed. Both spoke at the same time. 'The last victim was found in exactly the same way.'

'Right down to the red inscription of the word "Abeona" in the weave of the fabric,' added Fuz.

'Yes, that's what Dr Laos told us to expect when we spoke last night,' replied Anneka.

'Looks like we got ourselves a sick one here,' said Fuz, apparently to himself but Anneka replied anyway.

'Sick, maybe, but the fact that this is the first time, that we know of, that this killer has acted in six years would tell me that he knows what he is doing, that he plans and acts carefully. And that takes sanity, not insanity.'

'Are you a psychologist now?' asked Fuz, not realizing that Detective Constable Anneka Carlson had graduated with a first-class degree in psychology.

'No, I'm not. But it makes sense when you look at murder statistics that this guy is a psychopath, created by his experiences and not *sick* in the sense of being mentally ill.'

Fuz was impressed. 'Maybe you should come over and

work in forensics,' he said.

'Maybe, at some point,' she replied. 'But not now.'

'Why not?' asked Detective Constable Buzan.

'Let's just say I'm happy where I am,' answered Detective Constable Carlson.

Fuz understood her meaning. 'You mean that you're happy with Detective Inspector Roberts.'

'You said it, Fuz,' she replied. 'Besides, learning from the best is a rare opportunity and it was the inspector who taught me most of what I just said about killers being predominantly sane as opposed to insane.'

'I understand,' he said, before continuing. 'So, what's next, partner?' *Partner!* The word didn't sit well in Anneka Carlson's mind although she had to admit that in the short time they had been talking she got the feeling they would work well together.

'Well, let's start with seeing our witnesses. After that I suggest we try to meet Detective Inspector Roberts and Dr Laos, or at least have a conference call with them. And we need to check all missing person reports but let's do that together.'

'You got it. I think it's better if we make a start on that over here in my section rather than talking all day over the phone. Can you be here in about an hour's time?'

'I can,' she replied. 'That gives me time to send an email off to the detective inspector and let him know what we're doing. I'm also curious to know who is dealing with the press on this and if there's any sign of a press conference yet.'

'Well, I know that the press are all over the switchboard asking questions. We're not giving much away due to the fact that the victim is unidentified still and the last thing we want is the paparazzi finding the link with the previous case

. . . yet,' added Fuz, knowing that the media could be of great help when the time was right.

'In either case, I suspect Morti will be the press liaison when the time is right.'

Despite the fact that the station had its own specialized press liaison cops, those who knew Morti well knew that he liked to be seen in such cases as this. He figured it gave the public a sense of security to see the big cheese at the helm. *He might be right,* Buzan concluded mentally.

'Records indicate that the press back then were quick to seize on the hydrogen peroxide aspect of the murder, affectionately calling the case "peroxide homicide".'

It certainly sounded like a catchy headline for the press. Detective Constable Anneka Carlson noted the name and drafted an email to all parties, querying whether the peroxide in the current case could be definitively linked to the untraceable peroxide used previously.

Chapter Seven

Sunday 9 October, 8.10 a.m.,
Central Manchester Mortuary

Dr Karen Laos arrived at her place of work a little after 8 a.m. The rain had abated over the course of the morning and, although the atmosphere remained thick and heavy with fog, there were fleeting moments of hazy sunshine peeping through the clouds. It did little to take the chill away. *Damn autumnal fog*, Karen thought as she clicked the central locking on her car and headed to the side entrance of the mortuary, where she would key-swipe her way in past security. *The type of fog that one feels right in one's bones.*

She noted the Suzuki wagon that was Maxwell's car, parked opposite to hers. She also recognized Robert's somewhat beaten-up Cavalier, which he had parked nonchalantly against the far wall.

This means I'm the last one here in my own office, she thought, hurrying her pace past the security door. Roger had left by now. The daytime watch was held by several security cameras and a receptionist at the front desk. The receptionist, Maria, would see Karen's entrance register on the digital personnel recording system. *So much money on security and none left for a decent coffee machine.* More careful this morning than she had been the previous evening, Karen timed the action of using the on-off button perfectly. The coffee was far from the quality she drank at home but it worked all the same. She waved a polite good morning at Maxwell as she passed him in the mortuary en route to her office. She expected the blood results to be back by now and urgently wanted to confirm her suspicions.

'Good morning, Dr Laos,' came Inspector Roberts' familiar voice from behind her own desk.

The sight of him sitting in her chair took her aback slightly.

'Hello, Inspector, I see you beat me here.' Her sentiment also conveyed the message: *I see you made yourself at home.*

'I'm sorry, Doctor,' Detective Inspector James Roberts replied, having caught the subtext of her greeting. 'I was trying to access my emails as this phone is so bloody confusing, I can't ever seem to get my emails working properly.' He held his work-issued Blackberry high in the air as he spoke.

Karen couldn't help but smile.

'Let me take a look at it for you,' she said, offering her hands out in gesture.

Inspector Roberts eagerly passed his mobile device over the desk to Karen, adding, 'Whatever happened to plain simple Nokias? I was quite happy *not* having to read emails from my phone, but the powers-that-be insisted and now we all have these damned devices.'

After the click of a few buttons, Karen passed him his mobile back, adding, 'All done, Inspector.'

'*That* quickly? What did you do?' asked Roberts. .

'Quite simple, really. You had forgotten to enable

auto-updates of your work emails. Now your phone will synchronize with the police email exchange and update emails every twenty minutes to your device.'

Clearly impressed, Roberts thanked Karen. 'That saves me the embarrassment of a visit to the tech guys.'

They both smiled.

'If you think a Blackberry is tough to understand, try an HTC,' added Karen.

'What's an HTC?' asked Roberts.

'Maybe you would rather not know,' replied Dr Laos, smiling.

As Roberts studied his phone, now auto-updating a backlog of emails, Dr Laos pulled up a chair. She was still on the wrong side of her desk and didn't feel completely comfortable about it but she told herself there would be time to check her work emails later.

'Inspector,' she said, 'until we have an update on the blood results, there is little more I can tell you at this stage with regards to our victim that is going to help with your investigation.'

Was she trying to push him away? The thought crossed Roberts' mind.

'I understand, Dr Laos, but we are a team until further notice and I assumed that meeting here would be the best place to start. Besides, I would like to see our victim.'

Karen understood.

'Of course, and as you said, we are a team.' The words made her feel apprehensive. 'However, if you don't mind, I do need to get to my desk to check emails.'

'You mean to say that you don't have a phone that does that for you?' answered Detective Inspector Roberts, half sarcastically.

He was pleased to see the smile on Karen's face.

'Well, despite my impressive efforts just now with your phone, I prefer to see emails on a real computer screen in front of me. Call me old-fashioned.'

'That,' said Detective Inspector Roberts, moving out of her chair, 'is not a word I would use to describe you. I think you'll see an email from Detective Constable Carlson. She says she's with Detective Constable Buzan and they are making a start later with interviewing the witnesses who found the body. She has copied us all into her email. She has also sent an email asking whether we could trace the hydrogen peroxide back to case AA-262.'

'Yes, I see,' replied Dr Laos, now established in her email exchange. 'I'll reply now. And with regard to the constable's question, yes, it is possible.'

As she clicked on a desktop icon opening her typed initial findings of yesterday, she scanned through to 'collected samples'.

'The material in which the body was found was sent, as you know, to your own forensic division, so there is little I can do until they come back to us with their findings and any clues. However, the trace elements of hydrogen peroxide I found in the area of the victim's rectum are −' She paused as she calculated her findings with the help of her onscreen forensics wizard '– from a batch produced approximately fifteen years ago.'

'How do you know that?' asked Roberts.

'Simple, really; I placed the trace elements in analysis before I left here yesterday. The composition of the trace elements has been studied by a specialist piece of equipment we have called GVDMD.'

She smiled again as she noted Roberts' puzzled expression

and thought it might be fun to play with his understanding a little longer. 'Put in simple terms, Inspector: Gaseous Vapour Decontamination and Maturity Detector.'

'You call that simple, Dr Laos?' asked Detective Inspector Roberts.

He realized that she was playing with him slightly and smiled in submission.

'Please, explain what that is.'

'It is a very advanced piece of technology that is able to tell me the approximate age of any given substance, in this case hydrogen peroxide. The technology underlying the machine detects the extent of decontamination and computes an approximate age of manufacture as a result. It saves the likes of me from having to work through numerous complicated equations and delivers the result in a matter of hours, rather than days. It also means that we, as a team, are in a far stronger position than we were six years ago. Of course, I cannot tell you the batch from which the substance derived, but it gives us a good starting point in identifying manufacturers of this substance from fifteen years ago. Each batch is unique, in the same way that on appearance our fingers are similar but when subjected to finger-printing methods are uniquely individual.'

Detective Inspector James Roberts was grateful for the explanation and quite impressed. 'Complicated mobile phones and complicated GVDMDs.'

Karen stifled a laugh. He continued.

'Let's send this data over to the detectives in forensics and they can start detecting.'

Dr Laos opened the email that contained the case reports from AA-262. She studied it for a long while and found what she was looking for.

'Inspector, the pathologist that held this position before me passed away shortly after he retired. However, the case reports indicate that he was able to age-detect, the old-fashioned way, the hydrogen peroxide and placed it then at approximately nine years of age. I would therefore say that we are certainly looking at the same batch of hydrogen peroxide.'

Dr Laos had worked alongside Dr Albert Humes but he had been her senior and therefore taken the lead, and there were aspects that she had, by necessity of workload, been excluded from participating in. Maybe that was why she had felt a sense of failure.

'Which means,' said Roberts, 'that whoever has this substance either uses it very sparingly or has a great deal of it in storage. That also means that at some point approximately fifteen years ago a large order was placed for hydrogen peroxide, a fact which is going to help us in our investigations. It would have been before the age of internet buying, so somebody would have had to have gone to a manufacturer and purchased it in person. Whether that was our killer or whether he acquired the same batch afterwards will be determined with time.'

Detective Inspector Roberts took out his mobile phone to send a quick email over to the forensic detectives.

'I'll reply to Carlson for you and state that with the help of your wondrous machinery you have been able to infer that we are looking at the same hydrogen peroxide that was found six years ago.'

Dr Laos nodded her head to indicate her agreement. The upside to all this technology meant that at all times Dr Laos, Detective Inspector Roberts, Detective Chief Inspector Morti, Detective Constable Carlson, Detective Constable Buzan, the forensic response unit and even the as-yet unmet forensic psychologist, Trevor Stephenson, were all party to any emails sent, therefore keeping everyone updated on any findings.

Dr Karen Laos continued scanning through her inbox until she reached the email she was looking for. It had been sent at 6 a.m. and was from her colleagues in blood analysis, who had worked through the night. There was no message in the email text but that didn't matter. The attachment in PDF format was what Karen was looking for. She opened it up and saw the heading 'MBL', which stood for Manchester Blood Laboratory, with the sub-title, 'chemical analysis of blood and other human biological samples'. They had used the same case identification number that Karen had initiated, 'AD-482'. That was standard procedure for all multi-disciplinary teams when engaged in cross-service investigations so that all involved, whether in the police, in forensics, in psychology or pathology, would be speaking and reading from the same page.

'Inspector,' she said, drawing Roberts' expression to her own, 'our victim's blood is indeed positive for benzodiazepines, specifically the drug clonazepam, also known by its trade name Rivotril, or Klonopin, depending on where you are based in the world. This is the same drug that was found in case AA-262. Our victim's blood shows extremely high levels of the compound. I would guess that he was administered the drug for twenty-four hours, at a dose of two milligrams every three hours.

'This drug is available only as a tablet, so our victim would have been awake for the first dose for sure. That suggests that the drug was secreted in a drink, although it is not that easily dissolvable, but certainly possible. Thereafter, our killer would have had to force-feed the drug, possibly by tilting the victim's neck and pouring a drink with the tablet down his throat.'

Karen demonstrated the motion with her hands, without realizing it herself.

'Sixteen milligrams of this drug would be enough to cause a large adult male to fall into a near-coma state. You may want to make a note,' she added, 'it has been available since the 1970s and it has an unusually long elimination half-life of up to fifty hours, meaning that our victim would have last been administered with this drug possibly on Friday morning. You can therefore assume that our victim was given this drug at the very earliest Thursday 6 October, early morning. It may have been administered for a longer period but we can only judge that upon the drug's half-life and of course depending on when the time-frame comes to light that the victim was taken. I would surmise that time of death occurred anytime between midday and early evening Friday 7 October.

'This also fits with my initial impressions upon examination of the strangulation marks found on the victim's respiratory tract. If it's any consolation, although our victim would have been aware of his final moments, he would have been heavily sedated and cognitively impaired. A normal therapeutic dose of this drug would be between 0.08 and 0.2 milligrams per kilogram of body weight. Children come in all different shapes and sizes. Our victim is five foot two inches tall and had a maximum weight of fifty-one kilograms. Therefore, even a therapeutic dose would have caused drowsiness and disorientation. He would have been incoherent at the dose range detected in the blood.'

Detective Inspector Roberts quickly sent another email to all parties confirming that the same drug had been used as in case AA-262. He also clarified the time-frame in which Dr Laos thought the victim would have died.

'This means, Dr Laos, that if death occurred in the time-frame you have indicated, it is more than likely that the killer would have had to have disposed of the body any time after five in the afternoon on Friday. He would have known that by then it would be dark, given that we are in October, and therefore the chances of his being spotted were reduced. Now, the question we need to look at is one of geography.'

Karen listened attentively, finding herself in the unusual role of being on the end of someone else's deliberations.

'If we assume that at best guess the victim died at midday Friday, we have to also assume that the killer knew how much time he needed to move the body from wherever it is that he killed him, to the park. His timing was well thought out.'

Detective Inspector Roberts lifted his mobile phone and put a call through to the forensic psychologist Trevor Stephenson.

He used the hands-free function so that Dr Laos would be able to hear the conversation through the speaker phone. As Karen listened to Roberts relay the findings so far, she turned her gaze back to the laboratory blood results and noticed for the first time something that she had failed to see on initial review. She waited while Roberts spoke to the psychologist, and listened with interest.

'So, Trevor, given the information I have told you and that which you have read on your emails, what are your thoughts regarding the geography of our killer?'

Trevor's voice was husky, as if he smoked too many ciga-rettes a day, and Karen heard a wheeze when he paused between his words.

'I would say that this killer would need somewhere

extremely private to do what he does. I would assume that any type of change in his routine upsets him. He doesn't like to be interrupted and values his isolation. To this end, he would certainly need his own vehicle and would have finalized his murder in his own residence, away from public scrutiny. Therefore, to answer your geography question, I would assume that the killer lives, at furthest range, a five and a half hour drive away. That should help you pinpoint a locality to start your search.'

Detective Inspector Roberts let out an exasperated groan.

'Five and a half hours at maximum in any direction from Saline Park in Manchester would take us all the way up to the borders and further of Scotland, in the north, right down to London, in the south, across the North Sea in the middle of nowhere to the east and all the way to the furthest coast of Wales in the west.

'Thank you, Trevor, but I have a gut feeling that our killer knows this area very well and is therefore much more local. You said yourself that he values his privacy and doesn't like change. I can't see him driving more than five hours just to dispose of a body. That wouldn't fit with the profile we are looking at.'

'I'm just offering you some thoughts,' replied the psychologist. 'But I agree now that we are thinking aloud that this killer is a local. If not local, he lives within an hour, possibly two at a stretch. I also wanted to discuss with you the meaning of the word "Abeona" that the killer has been so careful to inscribe in the garments he wrapped the victims in.'

'There I have been taxed,' replied Detective Inspector Roberts. 'I understand the *meaning* of the word, but not the reason why he is using it. I would appreciate your thoughts.'

'Well, you can look at this in different ways. Belief in

a supernatural deity is not in itself evidence of any kind of mental disturbance, be it one of illness or one of personality. Every day people of all faiths gather in churches, mosques, cathedrals, synagogues, etc. Their belief in their own supernatural god is simply part of their mental makeup and can indeed be a positive marker of their unique individuality.

'However, looking at this in my position as a forensic psychologist, I have to assume that our killer's belief in this deity he calls Abeona is going to be key to our understanding of his development and, moreover, the fact that he is using this deity's name as a part of his killing suggests that it has become a driving force in the murders themselves. It represents something we are not yet aware of; possibly a metaphor our killer has developed and is enacting to represent the changes he craves in himself or in the world.'

Trevor wheezed in conclusion. Dr Karen Laos was still listening although what she had just read on the blood results was occupying her thoughts too. She waited to share her findings a while longer as Detective Inspector Roberts and Trevor Stephenson finished their call.

'OK, thanks, Trevor,' said Detective Inspector Roberts, adding, 'and please be sure to check your emails – we will keep you in copy.'

'I will do, Inspector. And if any more thoughts come up, I will let you know,' he replied.

As Detective Inspector Roberts turned his phone off from its hands-free mode, he waited for Dr Laos to speak, but she said nothing. It was then that he noticed that she seemed distant.

'Dr Laos, what did you think of my conversation with the psychologist?'

Karen gathered her thoughts.

'It was very interesting, Inspector, but there is something else.' Her words were laced with intrigue.

'Something else?' he asked. 'Such as?'

'From the blood results,' she said slowly. 'You remember when I said that I had found signs of an intravenous injection along the inner side of our victim's arms?'

'Yes,' he replied, anticipating her response.

'Well, the blood report from MBL has identified the contents of that IV.'

Detective Inspector Roberts froze as he listened to Karen's words.

'The lab technician has confirmed that our victim was injected with hydrogen peroxide.'

Roberts lifted his eyes in dismay, concluding aloud, 'That is different from last time.'

'Quite so,' agreed Dr Laos, the agitation evident in her voice too.

'This means that our earlier suspicion that the killer may change his pattern is correct,' said Detective Inspector Roberts. 'Why would he inject hydrogen peroxide into the veins of our victim?'

Karen looked blank as she contemplated the use of hydrogen peroxide.

'As I said before, it can be used as a cleanser as well as a preservative.'

'Well, I don't think that our killer was gently cleaning his victim,' added Detective Inspector Roberts.

He came to his worst realization, as yet unspoken, but one which both he and Dr Laos had shared.

'Goddamn it, Karen, he's preserving his kills.' *Karen.* That was the first time she had heard him call her by her given name.

'But why go to all the hassle to inject hydrogen peroxide into his victim when he hasn't even kept the body?' she asked. 'All we know is that he removed a superficial layer of the victim's skin.'

Roberts nodded, adding, 'I think he is practising. Even though he didn't keep the body of the victim, the change in the killer's behaviour would indicate that he is experimenting, even enhancing his ritual. If he kept the piece of skin, he would need hydrogen peroxide to preserve it in, right?'

Karen looked deep in thought.

'Well, yes, certainly to clean the so-called trophies, he would need the peroxide, but to preserve them I would think he is using something else, such as a type of formaldehyde fixative. However, it is no longer commonly available and was replaced by Formalyn because it was found to be carcinogenic.'

Dr Laos turned back to her computer screen and further reviewed the lab technician's report on the hydrogen peroxide.

'Our lab technician has added some additional notes. She states that H_2O_2 has been used recently by cosmetic companies as a so-called "cure" for acne, of course in lower strengths. I personally wouldn't touch the stuff, but apparently some people do and the trend towards its manufacture for these purposes is increasing. Our lab tech has drawn attention to this because she has seen, during the course of her work, some accidental toxicity in blood analysis that she has worked with over the past few years. As far as I know, death by direct hydrogen peroxide injection is extremely rare, which is, I think, why the lab technician has added these additional notes.'

Karen positioned herself to read the technician's report aloud for Detective Inspector Roberts' benefit.

'H_2O_2 injections possess dangerous qualities and therefore dangerous side-effects. High blood levels of H_2O_2 can create oxygen bubbles that block normal blood flow and can cause gangrene and death.'

Karen stopped.

'Well, there are no signs of gangrene and I still stick to my original assertion that the primary cause of death was strangulation.'

She returned to the lab technician's report.

'Destruction of blood cells has also been reported following intravenous injections of H_2O_2.'

As she spoke, Detective Inspector Roberts was back on his Blackberry emailing the latest update to all professionals involved in the case. He wanted to ensure that everything he and Dr Laos discussed was readily available to all professional parties. *Maybe his inability to use his phone earlier had been a ruse designed to open the morning*, Dr Laos thought. He certainly wasn't hesitating in using his device now.

Roberts stood up, approached Karen and spoke.

'You were right all along with what you said last night. Our killer is a trophy hunter.'

Karen corrected him.

'I didn't say he *was*. I simply stated a possibility.'

Karen typed some notes. Primary cause of death: manual strangulation. Secondary cause of death: massive benzodiazepine overdose. Tertiary cause and other contributory factors: severe physical and psychological trauma, toxicity poisoning by hydrogen peroxide. She concluded 'wrongful death' and forwarded her notes to all concerned parties.

'I suggest, Karen, that we go and see the victim's body now.'

She wondered why he would want to when all of the available evidence was readily available to him.

'I can go alone, Karen,' he said. 'I don't actually need to see the victim for any official reason. Call it antiquated but it's just something I feel I should do.'

Karen found herself admiring his humanity.

'It's not antiquated, Inspector. It's actually a breath of fresh air. Most of the police that come in here are only here to watch the autopsy process or to make an identification on the deceased with the victim's family.'

'That,' he said, referring to the identification process, 'is not something we are any closer to doing yet than we were yesterday.'

He hoped that Anneka Carlson and Detective Constable Buzan would be able to move that aspect of the enquiry further along as the day progressed.

Dr Laos called in Maxwell and, after exchanging some professional pleasantries, asked him to take Detective Inspector Roberts to see the victim. She returned to her computer screen as they left the room to make sure she hadn't missed anything else from the blood reports. The tragedy of the murder did not go unnoticed in her mind as Karen sat alone.

An otherwise healthy eleven-year-old boy who had had his life ahead of him now lay dead in her mortuary, for no good reason she could think of. Except there was a reason, she reminded herself, and that was far more terrifying than the murder itself. The murder was only the physical consequence of a killer who had by necessity developed a secret, inner fantasy life.

Karen Laos had been thinking a lot more than she usually did about the psychology of a killer over the past twenty-four hours. She had reasoned that it was because she had been spending so much time around Detective Inspector Roberts and the rest of his team, but that wasn't the only reason, she realized now as she sat alone in her office. This felt personal. In order to catch this killer, both she and Detective Inspector Roberts would need to start thinking like a killer, thinking about why he did what he did and about what excited and what upset him.

When she next looked up, Detective Inspector Roberts was back in the room.

'Thank you, Karen, for giving me the chance to see our victim,' he said quietly.

Both remained silent, interrupted only when the inspector's mobile started ringing.

'DI Roberts here,' he said sharply as he answered the call. He hadn't checked the caller identification, so deep in thought he had been after viewing the young victim's body.

'James, it's Paula,' said a female at the end of the line.

Detective Inspector Roberts felt slightly guilty. Detective Inspector Paula Stubs worked with Detective Constable Buzan and he'd known her for at least twelve years. He liked and respected Paula Stubs.

'Paula, I'm sorry, I didn't see your name and number on the phone,' he said apologetically.

'No need to apologize, James. I'm calling you regarding the material that Dr Laos sent over to us.'

Roberts mouthed the word 'forensics' to Karen as he listened to what Paula had to say.

'I have some good news for you, James. We have been able to identify the yarn from which the grey towelled gown was made.'

Roberts shot an excited wink in Karen's direction and

put his mobile phone to speaker mode before answering his colleague.

'That's great news, Paula, thank you.'

'Well, it's certainly a start,' Paula agreed. 'In fact, the killer has helped us without realizing it.'

'How so?' asked Roberts, eager to hear what his friend and colleague had to say.

'As you know,' she answered, 'we kept the material from six years ago in which victim AA-262 was found but we had no leads on it at the time.'

'Yes, I remember,' said Roberts. 'We were unable to identify the material conclusively because it was so unusual.'

'Not just unusual, James, but extremely rare. This time, however, we have a second identical item of clothing and the team has been able to identify the yarn as a result. I suggest you come over so we can talk about this in person,' she concluded.

Dr Laos signalled her willingness to head over with Roberts to the forensic response unit.

'OK, Paula, I'll be there in approximately an hour.' He checked his watch and saw that the time was already 9.15. 'I'm bringing Dr Karen Laos with me also.'

'OK, that's great, I'll see you then,' said Paula, ending the conversation.

'I think we should start making a move,' Roberts said to Karen after he had closed his mobile phone.

'That's fine with me. Which car shall we take?'

She saw the inspector's face light up like a small child.

'I wouldn't mind taking a ride in your sporty little BMW.' His response sounded both like an answer and a question wrapped together. Karen picked up her folder, paperwork and bag, and slipped her mobile phone in the front pocket of her knee-length jacket.

As they walked out of Karen's office, Detective Inspector Roberts sneaked a look at her navy blue dress and tight jacket. She was dressed to impress today. The thought stayed in his mind as he followed her out of the building and they made their way to her car.

Chapter Eight

Sunday 9 October, 9.30 a.m.

As he walked into the greenhouse that was fixed onto the
side of what had been his parents' 'playroom', he studied the
room around him. The glass above him and on all sides was
cracking and discoloured. The dark mould that grew from
the outside had been there for as long as he could recall.
He spent a lot of time in this room, moving objects from his
cellar to the greenhouse, usually several times a year, but as
it was his favorite month, October, a month that came around
annually but only every six years in terms of its importance
in his mind, he was here on a daily basis.

The hazy sunshine that slipped through the overcast sky
above provided very little warmth in what would otherwise
have been a cosy winter hideaway. He used this room for
other purposes, however. The floor was clear of any carpets
or rugs. Concrete and stone comprised the basis of the
structure of the floor. One dark wooden rocking chair from
1936 sat in the far easterly corner. The brand name, which
was emblazoned into the lower rung of the chair's left leg,
read 'William'. It had been chosen by his grandmother to

commemorate his father's birth.

His father had, prior to his death, often sat in this chair, passing away his latter years. The addition of his grandmother's spinning wheel, the walking wheel, had appeared after his father's death, carefully brought up from the bowels of the cellar beneath the house and lovingly restored. Spindle based, the wheel had played an important role in the development of his grandmother's hand-made gowns and other items of clothing, as too had the yarn she had chosen. The model was designed specifically as a device to rotate the spindle. He had been pleased to find that the yarn was ample in supply.

His grandmother had made several trips to Wales in order to locate the fibre preparation that was especially suitable to the walking wheel's long-draw spinning method. He had self-taught himself in recent years to master the technique of it, holding the yarn in his left hand as his right hand worked the wheel, which stood one and a half metres high.

He enjoyed the trance-like state he entered as the large wheel drove the much smaller spindle assembly, the spindle hypnotically revolving many times for each turn of the drive wheel. His arms had become muscular as a result of the many hours he had spent using this piece of equipment, the yarn spinning at a curious angle off the tip of the spindle, slowly storing itself around it.

He took pleasure and satisfaction in tying the large length of waste yarn onto the base of the spindle, spiralling it to the tip, overlapping a handful of fibre, his left hand holding gently onto it. His right hand slowly and meticulously turned the drive wheel clockwise, simultaneously walking backwards and drawing the fibre in his left hand at an angle away from the spindle. He had perfected the motion of using his left hand to control the tension on the wool, thus producing an even result. *My grandmother would be proud.* He so wanted someone to be proud of his achievements. '*I always have Abeona,*' he told himself, as he turned the wheel backwards a short distance, unwinding the spiral from around the spindle. He then quickly turned it clockwise once more, winding the newly made yarn onto the spindle, thereby finishing the wind-on by spiralling back out to the tip again to make another draw.

He studied his creation and knew that it would come in useful. It always did as he continued in his work, bettering himself. He placed it in the straw-knit basket that sat on the concrete floor and moved towards his large wooden storage cupboard that sat beneath a cracking window in the greenhouse. With his right hand, he opened the main double door and with his left pulled open a heavy drawer. From there he took a four-metre length of red yarn that he had created seven years ago.

He placed it in a circular pattern around the concrete floor. This was why he had cleared the room of all but the essentials. He returned to the storage cupboard, this time taking four large wooden bowls. Checking the four quarters of the circle he had created, he placed one in the north, one in the east, one in the south and one in the west. At the centre of the circle he placed a small wooden bench, not dissimilar to a workman's tool bench. Upon this he placed a glass jar. His hands trembling with excitement, he caressed the jar and studied its contents. On the outside he had wrapped a length of brown paper around the top of the jar's lid, sealing it down with a red elastic band. On top of the brown paper he had inscribed with ink, again in red, the word 'Abeona'.

The formaldehyde he had filled it with had changed from its original dark orange colour to a clearer, see-through solution. *'I have perfected the process of plastination,'* he told himself. He had discovered that plastination was the term given to his work. It was a technique or process used to preserve bodies or body parts, replacing water and fat, ensuring that the specimens could be touched, which he thoroughly enjoyed, did not smell or decay and would retain most of their original properties.

His father had left a vast haul of equipment in the cellar, which he had moved into a small dark adjoining room, and it was there that he would spend much of his time, following the four steps that ultimately resulted in plastination. Utilizing his formaldehyde solution, he would fixate the body parts that he had collected, carefully placing them in a bath of acetone which, when frozen, would draw out all the water remaining. He would then place his trophies in a bath of polyester, a liquefied polymer, which would create a vacuum, forcing the acetone to boil at a low temperature.

As the acetone vapourized, it would draw the polyester in behind it, leaving his trophy filled with a type of liquid plastic. It was a technique he that found difficult at first but now one which he had mastered and derived great pleasure from. The crowning moment in his work had always been in finally placing the trophy back into a jar of formaldehyde and sealing it forever, safe from intrusion.

As he studied the jar in front of him, at the centre of the circle he had created, he lifted it from the top of the bench, and with a motion less of a shake and more of a judder, he took pleasure in the sound of the solution sloshing around the firm piece of human skin, which he had removed from his most recent prop's body. He replaced the jar on the table and moved back to the storage cupboard, this time removing two bird feathers, a red candle, a small bottle of water that he had left beneath the early October moon-soaked night sky, and a large piece of rock. He reached for a box of matches and lit the candle.

In the bowl at the east of his red circle, he placed the bird feathers. In the bowl at the south he placed the burning red candle. In the bowl at the west of his circle he poured the water from its bottle, throwing it across the floor as he moved to the bowl at the north part of his circle. In this he placed the rock. He moved now to the east of his circle. He leant down and picked up the bowl with the bird feathers.

Raising it high above his head, he said aloud, 'I call upon the elements of the east, of air, of wind and of the power of flight to come unto me and be present here in this room.' He lowered the bowl to beneath his chin and continued, 'I bid you hail and welcome.'

Following the same process, he moved now to the south of his circle, reciting the words, 'I call upon the elements of the south, of fire and of passion to come unto me and be present here in this room.' He lowered the bowl to beneath his chin and continued, 'I bid you hail and welcome.'

He walked to the bowl in the west of his circle. He picked up the bowl containing his moon-blessed water and recited the words, 'I call upon the elements of the west, of water and of the great oceans to come unto me and be present here in this room.' He lowered the bowl to beneath his chin and continued, 'I bid you hail and welcome.'

He moved slowly now to the bowl at the northern end of his circle. He leant down to pick it up in the same way as he had with the others. It was heavier than the last three, the rock inside it weighing a little less than one kilo.

Lifting it above his head, his arm muscles twitching, he said, 'I call upon the elements of the north, of the earth and of stability and growth to come unto me and be present here in this room.' He lowered the bowl to beneath his chin and continued, 'I bid you hail and welcome.'

He moved assertively now to the centre of his circle.

He again picked up the jar with his latest victim's remains inside, and recited a short verse from memory.

'The purpose of this ritual is to call upon the goddess Abeona, to whom I have dedicated my life. Abeona keep me safe, Abeona help me find my way, Abeona let me feel you, Abeona let me be one with you. Abeona, through this gift I offer –' He signalled to his victim's remains '– my service and I pledge to continue my work in your name and gratefully accept your protection.'

Sunday 9 October, 10 a.m., Greater Manchester Police Headquarters, Forensic Response Unit

Detective Constable Anneka Carlson had sat for close to two hours with her counterpart Detective Constable 'Fuz' Buzan. The two were now on first-name terms although she was still none the wiser as to why he was known as Fuz. When she had arrived at his desk he was sitting at his computer delving through the national police database on missing persons, hoping to find a link to the victim in Dr Karen Laos's mortuary. Anneka Carlson had met Detective Constable Buzan only briefly before and did not recognize him at first glance. She figured that he probably had a couple of years on her with regard to his age and therefore experience.

He was well dressed in a slim-fit dark suit, minus a tie. He was about six feet tall, and had dark, well-maintained short hair and piercing dark brown eyes. She noticed his designer stubble and wondered to herself whether this was why he was called Fuz. Between carefully timed coffee breaks, the two had learnt a great deal about the missing persons database. Anneka had also been surprised and saddened to learn of the number of individuals currently listed as missing. The database pooled information from various sources, covering missing children, people missing abroad, child abduction and missing adults.

The system pulled its information from the statutory as well as the voluntary sectors although, as Fuz had explained to her when she arrived, only a police officer had the authority to enter data into the system. When an individual reported someone as missing to the police, the officer would take a statement regarding the person and enter additional information, including photos, details of the events that may have led to their disappearance, places the missing person was known to have visited and any relevant details about friends or relatives.

The system also had a clever DNA identifier function, which was enabled if a police officer had taken something that would contain the missing person's DNA, such as a toothbrush. The item with DNA would be sampled and, when a missing person was found, dead or alive, definitive proof would be available to link the missing individual to the deceased, or located, whatever the outcome may be. The database had been a relatively recent development in the government's drive for better integration and information-sharing across the UK's forty-three independent police forces. A police officer checking the database would now have access to all missing persons reports from across the country.

Detective Constable Buzan had explained to Anneka that from the time a new entry was made, it would take forty-eight hours for it to become live and available on the system. This meant that had their victim been entered into the system as missing, he should now be traceable. Of course, as Anneka had reminded Buzan, the only confirmed facts surrounding the victim so far were his approximate age and the circumstances under which he had died, as determined by Dr Karen Laos.

They still knew nothing about his background, his family or anything else pertinent. Identifying their victim relied entirely upon following clues until they reached a good potential fit. That was a lesson that Detective Inspector Roberts had taught her from day one. 'And we don't always figure it out,' he had told her. 'There are plenty of unsolved deaths every year.'

Now, as they sat together, Anneka in a spare chair positioned in full sight of Buzan's computer screen, they had searched the database on children who had been abducted and drawn a blank there with no results that fitted the profile of the deceased. They had agreed that starting with the abduction list would make sense as they wanted to eliminate the possibility that the victim had not gone willingly.

'We still have to check the part of the database that details children reported as missing in the more general sense,' said Anneka, hoping that there they would find something of use in their investigation.

'Well,' replied Fuz, 'we can get to that but first let's have a talk about the other things we have to do.'

'The importance of working from a map.' Carlson recalled the detective chief inspector's words.

'We have our lunchtime appointment with the students

who found the body.' Anneka checked her watch. The time was coming up to 11 a.m. 'I think we should take a look at the reports taken by uniform when they attended the scene where the body was found on Friday night,' she added, 'before we go blind into our meeting with the students.'

Fuz nodded his head. 'I have them here underneath all these files,' he said as he cleared his desk to reach the reports. 'I'll also print off some extra copies of the final report that was produced following case AA-262. The pathologist that worked on that case was a Dr Albert Humes, now deceased. Dr Laos would have worked with him, but according to the records was not in charge. We already know that Detective Inspector Roberts worked as the lead cop on the case.'

Anneka asked a question that had been on her mind for a while.

'Other than the fact that the body was not identified for over a year, were there any specific areas on which the investigation fell down?'

'Not especially; other than the fact that the killer was never found. The circumstances were identical to the present case, except that last time the killer dumped his victim in a different locality. We also know that with AA-262 he did not use hydrogen peroxide as an injection. However, it was found on the victim's body in sparing amounts.'

'So,' concluded Anneka, 'the superficial removal of the victim's skin has been seen in both cases, as has the fact that the victims were drugged with benzodiazepines in order to, we assume, incapacitate them. Strangulation was recorded as the primary cause of death in both victims and both victims also had their palatine tonsils removed and were found wrapped in identical home-made material.'

She was clarifying in her own head as well as

summarizing for Buzan's sake.

'That's correct,' he concurred. 'There is nothing else in the case report of AA-262 that stands out.'

'In that case,' replied Anneka, 'let's take a look at the witness statements from the students. And,' she added, 'later we need to go back to the missing kids database and speak to the detective inspector about checking out sellers of hydrogen peroxide.' She scanned her work emails on her mobile before continuing. 'I have a feeling he'll want to do that himself and check with the help of Dr Laos into the possibility of pinpointing out where our killer may be getting his hands on such large quantities of benzodiazepines.'

Anneka sent a quick email to Detective Inspector Roberts in this regard.

'Well, unless he is a prescription user, there are many other places he could obtain clonazepam, such as . . .' Buzan paused, his face full of thought. 'The internet from many illegal pharmacies.'

'It also has a street value,' added Anneka, 'which means that if he is buying it from users, it will be practically impossible to get a trace on that.'

They turned their attention to the witness statements, taken by their uniformed colleagues late on Friday night. Detective Constable Carlson instinctively picked up the paperwork on the female final-year student. Buzan picked up both of the statements given by the male students.

'Twenty-one years old, her name is Valerie Thomas,' began Anneka. 'Final-year law student. Uniformed report that she is originally from north London, moved here aged eighteen to start her studies. By all accounts she is a good student. The cop's observations were that she was cooperative throughout their questioning.'

'And?' asked Buzan. 'What do they say about the events that led to her being in Saline Park?'

Carlson looked at him briefly before continuing:

'She and her two friends had been out for the evening at a student bar on the edge of the campus's outer perimeter called The Antelope.'

'I know that place,' said Buzan, his voice somewhat excited, his facial expression lost in fond recollection.

Carlson suspected that he himself had been there as a student, but didn't probe any further.

'Valerie told uniformed that she left at the same time as her two male friends.'

'That makes sense seeing that they share the same house,' interrupted Buzan.

'Indeed. I know that if I were a lone female student walking back home at night, I wouldn't have walked through Saline Park.'

Buzan agreed. It would make sense to stick to well-lit populated areas. But then, as he had realized during the course of his career, people did not always think logically. He had certainly seen the consequences of such behavior during his time with CID.

'So,' he said, 'why did they decide to walk across the park rather than call a taxi?'

'That,' said Detective Constable Carlson, 'could have been for various reasons. Maybe they fancied a stroll in the park before heading home. Maybe they were simply clearing their heads after a night in a dark, overcrowded bar with, I am sure, more than a few drinks down their necks.'

Buzan smiled an affirmative understanding, one which told Anneka Carlson that he too had been in a similar predicament during his younger years. *But then hadn't they all?*

She suppressed her own recollections and continued reading.

'Uniformed say that although Valerie appeared slightly drunk, she was coherent and lucid considering the fact that it was she who –' She paused '– discovered the body.'

'Let me guess,' interrupted Buzan. 'She walked off the main track to relieve herself.'

'Spot on,' said Carlson. 'She said that she went far into the undergrowth, feeling conscious with her male friends laughing at her inability to hold her bladder.'

Buzan opened up the two brief reports he had in his hands. 'The two guys have corroborated her story to that point. Of course, the fact that she actually found the body is not something that they themselves were party to, being as they were some thirty metres from her by this point.' He thumbed through the sections of the reports until he reached the part he thought most salient. 'They both reported to uniformed officers that they heard a scream coming from Valerie's position and ran to see what was wrong. By the way, the two males have names.'

'*You don't say,*' Detective Constable Carlson found herself saying in her head but said nothing and let him continue.

'Both, as we know, are second-year students, studying arts and humanities. The first of the males who gave his statement goes by the name of Christopher Woods. He was apparently slightly ahead of his friend, whose name is Chuck Adams.'

'Chuck Adams?' asked Carlson. 'I suppose it's not such an unusual name, considering that you go by the preferred name of Fuz.'

Buzan looked slightly deflated but shot her a half-smile.

'Who made the 999 call?' asked Carlson.

'That,' said Buzan as he continued thumbing through the paperwork, 'was Mr Chuck Adams. Mr Woods was too busy trying to console Valerie.'

'Are you happy with what you have read?' Detective Constable Buzan asked Detective Constable Carlson.

'Happy?' she asked, puzzled.

'I mean, do you feel that we have covered the witnesses' statements to your satisfaction before we visit them?'

'I think so,' she replied, her eyes scanning the remainder of the document she held in her hands. 'I don't think we are going to learn a great deal more before we actually meet these people.'

Buzan agreed. 'Even then, we are only covering formalities by visiting the witnesses.'

Anneka looked at him before she replied to what he had said.

'That's true, but we also have a duty of care to these students. They did the right thing in reporting finding the body and, although they may not know it yet, the experience they went through on Friday night will stay with them for a long time.'

He lifted the phone on his desk and put a call through on extension 783 to one of the forensic scientists that had been working the crime scene. Julia Amos, an experienced scientist and investigator, answered the desk.

'Science division, Amos speaking.'

Buzan always thought that Amos sounded hurried in the way she spoke, as if there just weren't enough hours in the day for her to complete her work.

'Julia, it's Fuz.'

Anneka listened with interest at the manner in which her counterpart had introduced himself. *This is a guy that does not go for formalities*, she found herself thinking.

Buzan flicked his line to speaker phone for Carlson's benefit.

'Morning, Fuz, how's it going over there?' Amos spoke quickly.

'It's going pretty good. I'm here with Detective Constable Carlson – you're on the speaker phone.'

'That's fine with me. I guess you're calling to find out if we have anything for you from the crime scene?'

She didn't give Buzan the chance to reply. Carlson smiled.

'Well, what I can tell you is that the witnesses seem to check out from a forensics point of view. During processing the crime scene, we have been able to run a bit of trainer tracking; a kind of fingerprinting for footwear.'

She paused and clarified herself.

'Let me explain what I mean. Different makes and styles of trainers have their own tread patterns, which means that we have access to databases that reveal, for example, whether the prints we have taken from a crime scene are from a Nike Air Max or a Converse All Star brand, or indeed any other branded shoe type. All three of our witnesses were wearing trainers on Friday night. The young lady was wearing a pair of Adidas Sumbrahs and the two young men were both wearing Adidas Jeremy Scott Wings.

'Their choice of footwear also fits with research that tells us that the younger an individual the more expensive his or her choice in footwear is likely to be. We have confirmed that footprints from all three brands were found in the area of the crime scene. The young woman's prints were, as would be expected, closest to the victim's body.

'The pattern of her movement tells me that she left the main pedestrian dirt path and walked off to the left. Her prints continue for thirty metres, which fits with her version of events. Her walk to the undergrowth was what we might call zigzagged, suggesting that she was indeed looking for the best place to stop and pee. The prints left by the two males also fits with their version of events. The prints left by Mr Woods follow the same pattern as those left by Valerie, although the pace with which he walked was much faster. I would suggest that he was close to a jog with regard to his movement.'

'That,' said Buzan, 'would make sense if he were running to her aid. What type of distance can you place between his footprints?'

Amos did not pause before replying.

'Initially when he veered off the pedestrian track, his prints were at a distance of two feet apart, suggesting that he was walking to start with. However, as his prints approach Valerie's location, and that of the body, the space between his prints is paced at around a metre apart. That would suggest that by this point he was running.'

'That all fits with the testimony given by the group,' said Buzan.

Amos continued with her discourse.

'Now, regarding the tracks left by Mr Chuck Adams, they are all paced at a space of approximately one metre, suggesting that as soon as he left the pedestrian path, he was running.'

She paused.

'However, his tracks stop at sixteen metres closing in on the location of Valerie and Christopher.'

There was a brief moment of silence as Buzan flicked through the testimony left by Adams.

'That also fits with his description of the time and location from which he made the emergency call to 999.'

'Now,' continued Amos, 'that's the footprints of the witnesses. Unfortunately we have not found any other useable footprints in the precise area. Obviously we've had the patch closed off since the discovery of the body. The killer you're looking for had gone to careful lengths to disguise his movements. The most likely explanation is that he wore protective clothing on his footwear. Clearly, the body didn't just appear from nowhere.

'Which brings me onto my next point. You will be pleased to know that we have managed to find physical signs in the undergrowth that suggests that the body was dragged to its final location. On the downside, due to the bad weather and heavy rain in recent days, the pattern of dragging has been badly degraded and is patchy at best. I can't tell you from which direction the body came to find itself in the undergrowth, whether the perpetrator approached from the pedestrian path or came across the park in a vehicle. Either way he would have needed a vehicle to get to the park; forensic teams are continuing to search for tracks. I can update you later in this regard.'

Buzan clicked 'mute' on his phone briefly and asked Anneka, 'Is there anything else you want to know before we hang up?'

She shook her head.

'Thanks, Julia, you have been a great help. Do you mind putting all what you have told us into an email, making sure that everyone involved in the case is copied in?'

'I was about to do that just before you rang me,' she replied.

Of course you were, thought Detective Constable Buzan. *You're quicker than a mosquito.*

'And,' she added, 'I'll email over to you all the results of any tyre prints found in the vicinity of the victim. Give me until the afternoon for that.'

'Thank you, Julia, we'll speak later,' said Detective Constable Buzan, closing the line.

Chapter Nine

Sunday 9 October, 10.20 a.m.,
Greater Manchester Police Headquarters

Dr Karen Laos had parked her car in the parking space that
Detective Inspector Roberts had suggested, which was behind
the main building of the station. They had enjoyed chatting to
each other during their journey, Detective Inspector Roberts
admiring Karen's wheels and both relying less now on small-
talk to pass the time than they had previously. Karen had
learned that Roberts had been married until ten years ago,
when his wife had left him, citing irreconcilable differences,
which, Roberts had explained, she had persistently attributed to the time he dedicated to his job.

He had been polite and professional enough not to ask
too many prying questions about Karen's life, but she was
surprised to find herself volunteering certain aspects of it,
such as her formative years and her university education.
She had almost reciprocated his personal information about
his marriage and its subsequent break-up but they had run
short of time as she pulled her car into the parking area of
the station. Roberts checked them both in at front desk and

they started to walk across to the forensic response unit to meet with Detective Inspector Paula Stubs.

'Anneka and Detective Constable Buzan have been busy this morning,' said Karen as she checked her mobile phone.

'Indeed,' replied Roberts. 'They've made a good start. I had hoped they would have had some luck by now with the missing persons database, though. No doubt they will return to that as soon as they can. Let's see also what Julia Amos comes back with later with regard to the crime scene investigations.'

'Well, until then,' she said, the two of them now approaching the lift that would take them up to the main hub of the forensic response unit, 'let's go and speak to your friend Paula and see what she's got for us with regard to the fabric and yarn.'

My friend Paula? Roberts contemplated Karen's words, and noted that she had accentuated the words 'your' and 'friend'. Did he sense a touch of jealousy in her voice? He shrugged off his assumptions as being without basis. The lift door sprung open and they walked in, Detective Inspector Roberts pressing the button for the third floor. Their twenty-second trip up to the third floor stifled their conversation as they had an audience of officers and other personnel riding with them. Karen noticed how Detective Inspector Roberts greeted them all personally. He was clearly well known and much liked by all of his colleagues.

They exited the lift on the third floor and stepped out onto the now loud and noisy forensics floor. Detective Inspector Roberts could see neither Anneka nor Buzan and reasoned that he and Dr Laos must have narrowly missed them on their way in. Between the rows of uniform and bland partitioned desks, Detective Inspector Roberts spotted Paula

Stubs waving at them through the crowd.

She was making her way through two particularly tight aisles of desks, each one partitioned off with the same five-foot-five-inch screens. Detective Inspector Roberts had always hated the so-called 'cubicle desk'. Rather than maximize work space in cramped conditions, as had been their design purpose, he felt them to be impersonal and aloof. Row upon row of them remained in this section of the station, which had not been renovated or even given a lick of paint in years.

Roberts led Dr Laos in Paula Stubs' direction, reaching his hand out in a congenial greeting.

'Hello, Paula, how's life treating you?'

'Good, thanks, James, although as busy as always. Dr Laos, I assume?' she said, turning her glance in Karen's direction.

Karen immediately liked this woman and, as was the case with many officers of this division, knew that they had met somewhere in the past.

'Yes,' she replied. 'It's a pleasure to meet you, Inspector.'

Detective Inspector Stubs had the same body shape as Karen Laos and they looked remarkably similar, other than the fact that Karen's hair was dark brown while Paula's was jet-black, shoulder length and straightened.

'Please, call me Paula.'

'In that case, call me Karen,' reciprocated Dr Laos.

'Well, James, Karen, please follow me to my office and we can get started.'

Paula Stubs spoke with an authoritative edge to her voice and led the way through two more aisles of desks before reaching an individual office at the far end of the room. As she ushered Detective Inspector Roberts and Dr Laos in, closing the door behind them, the noise outside decreased to that of a background hum.

She had placed two additional chairs at her desk in readiness for her guests' arrival. Detective Inspector Roberts and Dr Laos sat down. The desk was a semi-circular shape, with a large PC sitting on the left side, elevated to prevent neck strain.

'As I said on the phone earlier, we were able to get a clear identification on the yarn used in the grey towelled gown in which both victims were dressed,' said Paula as she took the black swivel office chair behind her desk. 'I can add that we got extremely lucky on this one.'

Her face had become serious and concentrated indentations in her skin appeared as she continued.

'The towelling material of the gown itself is highly common and therefore looking for its origins would be like searching for the proverbial needle in the haystack. However, the intricate and carefully placed inscription of the word "Abeona" was where we got lucky. Our killer has used the exact same yarn on both occasions. I had archives pull out the gown in which victim AA-262 was dressed six years ago, as soon as this case came in late Friday night.'

She looked at Dr Laos.

'Thanks to your quick action in sending over the latest gown in the early hours of yesterday morning, we were able to spend yesterday in the lab studying the texture of both samples of the red yarn used for the inscription. Before the second victim appeared, the yarn sample from victim AA-262 had been classified as, what we call in forensic fibre analysis, "individual".

'This means that we had never come across the material before, nor seen anything like it. Now that we have a second, identical type of yarn, neither can be considered alone, to the exclusion of the other.'

Detective Inspector Roberts and Dr Laos both said that they understood.

Detective Inspector Paula Stubs continued.

'The various analytical methods available for fibre analysis yield different kinds of information. It is therefore desirable to select a combination of methods when analyzing such evidence. This ensures that we are able to optimize accuracy and precision. In the current case, we compared both samples with the use of a stereomicroscope, a comparison microscope and a compound light microscope, equipped with polarized light capability. By comparing the samples as "questioned sources" we have been able to determine that both are consistent with the assumption that they originated from the same source. We place a great level of value on the association found. Firstly, the fibre type is identical. Secondly, so is the fibre colour. Thirdly, the number of fibres within each given piece of yarn is identical. More importantly, however, is the fact that the tensile strength of the yarn is also identical. There is no way that these fibres could possibly have come from any other source, which led us to look for common denominators in the material's property.'

Detective Inspector Paula Stubs placed the fists of her hands under her chin and held a fixed stare at Detective Inspector Roberts and Dr Laos.

'Only fabric from the same source material possesses the same tensile strength.'

Detective Inspector Roberts could see the anticipation in Karen's face growing as Paula spoke.

'So, Paula, what can you tell us about the origins of where this yarn may have come from?' he asked.

'It's not just a case of what I can tell you about where this material *may* have come from,' she replied. 'I can tell you exactly where this yarn came from.'

She spoke with such a certainty to her words that the anticipation built even further.

'The fibre used is from an animal source, which is not that unusual in itself. Wool originating from sheep is after all the most commonly used animal fibre in textile production. The finer woollen fibres are used in the production of clothing, whereas the coarser fibres are found in carpet. The diameter and the degree of scale protrusion of the fibres are other important characteristics. Using reconstruction we have been able to determine that both the yarn found on the gown in which victim AA-262 was found six years ago and that found on our current victim originated from the same source; that is to say, that they were once a piece of the same continuous source material.'

Detective Inspector Roberts let out an impressed breath of air.

'That is excellent work, Paula. I assume that because you have been able to tell us where the yarn originated, you can you tell us from where the wool originates?'

Detective Inspector Paula Stubs smiled an affirmative *yes* in response to Detective Inspector Roberts' question and Karen thought she caught a wink.

'Indeed I can, James. As I said previously, it is in part thanks to our killer's use of the same material in the two cases that has allowed us to identify the wool's origin. The yarn derives from a type of wool, one so rare that the sheep species from which it comes was once thought to be extinct. Have you heard of Balween?'

Both Dr Laos and Detective Inspector James Roberts said

no at the same time.

'Nor would I expect you to have,' replied Paula. 'It is a Welsh word meaning "white blaze". The body of this species of sheep is dark grey, black or brown and is the only native British sheep species with white colouring on the face, socks and tail.'

'Clearly our killer would have dyed the wool in order for it to appear red,' interjected Karen. 'Any leads on that aspect?'

Paula thought for a short moment before replying.

'I'm afraid not. The dye appears to be of a very common mass-produced type, which we would not be able to correctly identify. However, you will be pleased to hear that this species of sheep is native to only a spattering of regions in Wales.'

She checked her notes for what seemed to be the first time during this meeting.

'Namely, Cardigan, Brecon and Carmarthen. I can also confirm that the age of the wool used in both yarn samples is approximately seventy years old.'

'Then that means two things,' said Roberts, his mind drifting as he mentally explored the possibilities that Paula's findings would lead to in regard to the ongoing investigation. 'Firstly, that somebody in around about the year 1935 would have had to have made a number of trips to one of these regions in order to buy the wool and secondly that this is where we need to start looking.'

'Indeed,' said Paula, adding, 'I suggest that you start looking for farmers with specialist knowledge of this sheep species as our research tells us that after a particularly harsh winter back in the 1940s only one male Balween was said to have remained. Therefore, it is entirely due to the hard efforts of farmers in the regions mentioned that this species is now alive and thriving, although it is still classified as endangered.'

'Paula,' said Roberts, 'you have been invaluable. We owe you.'

He gestured his gratitude with an arched wave of his right hand.

'You're welcome any time, James,' she replied.

Detective Inspector Roberts and Dr Laos left the office and headed in the direction of the division's cafeteria, which was more of a converted storage room with a few plastic tables and chairs and a self-service coffee- and tea-making facility. Both chose coffee and pulled some seats up along a table, which looked like it had seen many debates around it over the years.

Dr Laos checked her watch and was surprised to see it was already 11.30.

'We were in there for an hour?' she asked.

'Give or take,' replied James. 'But we did get an excellent result.'

'Finally,' agreed Karen, 'and hopefully somewhere to start from in trying to catch this guy.'

She had spoken like a cop. Detective Inspector Roberts smiled his approval.

'Are you ready for a trip, Karen?' he asked.

She had seen this coming when Detective Inspector Paula Stubs had mentioned the areas in Wales where they could start their investigations.

'To Wales?' she clarified.

'Yes, it seems like the best place to make our next move.'

Karen found, somewhat to her surprise, that she did not hesitate in agreeing.

'Sure. When do we leave?'

'We should make a move early this evening.' He checked his BlackBerry. 'Before then we need to start on identifying some sellers of hydrogen peroxide that were in business a decade and more ago, as well as have a think about where our killer has been getting his benzodiazepines. Anneka sent an email asking whether we would follow this up.'

She confirmed his thoughts before he had the chance to ask her.

'I know an excellent chemist, about half an hour from here. She should be able to help us in accessing that kind of information.'

'Then', he said, finishing the last drops of coffee in his cup, 'I suggest we make a move. We have plenty to do.'

Sunday 9 October, midday,
Mulme Hall student residence, Victoria Park, three
miles from Greater Manchester Police Headquarters

Valerie Thomas paced nervously up and down the length of the apartment she shared with Christopher Woods and Chuck Adams. She peered out from the curtains that draped across the window frame overlooking the main road, the park itself on the other side. Woods and Adams were both sitting on the sofa playing on their Xbox.

'How can you two just sit there so calmly?' asked Valerie, wringing her hands in anticipation of the cops' arrival. 'And stop playing that bloody game, it's so inappropriate!' she added, as she reached for the remote control, promptly closing down the violent game they were halfway through.

'Hey!' exclaimed Chuck. 'Why did you do that?'

'Because,' she replied, 'if you haven't forgotten, there are two murder squad cops coming over any time to see *us*.'

'What are you so worried about?' asked Christopher, standing up from the sofa. 'It's not as if we've done anything wrong.'

Valerie, usually a model of composure and togetherness, now seemed completely on edge.

'We may not have done anything wrong, but . . .' She paused. 'I don't know, I just can't get the image of that body out of my mind. And,' she added, 'the two of you playing that game where you're shooting cops to death doesn't help.'

'It's just a game, Val,' said Chuck. 'It helps us think about normality.'

Valerie looked maddened.

'Normality? If you want normality why don't you try opening your textbooks once in a while and doing some studying?'

'There's plenty of time for that,' replied Christopher.

'You won't be saying that when you get to your third year,' said Valerie moodily.

She sat down, trying to steady her nerves.

'What do you think they want to ask us?'

Both Chuck and Woods picked up on their chance to ease her nerves.

'It's just formality, Val,' said Chuck, placing his hand on her shoulder. 'You should know that, you're the law student.'

'Besides,' interjected Christopher, 'we have already gone over everything we know to the uniformed guys.'

Chuck nodded. 'Exactly, and not just once, but twice now.'

'Don't remind me,' said Valerie, standing up.

'Why did they send the uniformed cops around again this morning?' She shuddered as she continued. 'After all we went through, standing there for two hours in the middle of

Saline Park on Friday night.'

'It's just a tactic they use,' said Christopher, sounding more confident than he actually felt. 'It means they have nothing to go on and want to rattle anything out of us they think we haven't told them already.'

His voice was full of trepidation. He knew that he actually had no clue what he was talking about. Valerie and Chuck knew it too but said nothing. Valerie felt grateful that her room-mates were at least trying to put her at ease. She checked out of the window again.

The tremor returned in her voice. 'Oh God, I think they're here.'

Chuck and Christopher joined Valerie at the window, Chuck confirming her suspicions.

'Yep, I think that's them, one guy, and one woman. Both smartly dressed.'

It hadn't taken long for Detective Constable Anneka Carlson and Detective Constable Buzan to reach Victoria Park, one of Manchester's most popular residential locations for students attending the city's university, but they had set out earlier than planned as both had felt hungry. An ideally located Starbucks a few minutes from the station had given them both the chance to eat. Carlson had selected a hot tuna panini, while Buzan had gone for a chicken salad sandwich. Both had had a latte, Anneka's without sugar, Buzan's with one.

Now, as Buzan pulled his car alongside 8, Upton Road, he looked out of his window and saw the three faces peering down at them.

'I think we're here,' he said to Anneka, smiling with amusement at the students.

As Anneka stepped out of the passenger side of the car,

she stole a glance upwards towards the window, clocking the expressions on their faces. Anneka took the lead and walked slightly in front of Buzan. She knocked on the front door.

Upstairs, Valerie said 'Here we go' and Chuck took the initiative to walk along the hallway and down the stairs to answer the front door. Holding her CID badge in her left hand, Detective Constable Carlson introduced herself.

'Good morning. I am Detective Constable Carlson and this is my partner, Detective Constable Buzan.' She moved her head to the right to indicate Buzan's presence as she said his name. Buzan stepped forward.

'I assume you are either Mr Woods or Mr Adams?'

'Chuck Adams,' replied the tall blond-haired student. 'Please, come on in.'

As she stepped into the narrow passageway, Anneka found herself taken back more than a decade in time, recalling the same smell and house shape that she had lived in as a student. *Teen Spirit*. The title of Nirvana's hit song sprung into her mind.

Adams led the way along the passageway and up the flight of sixteen stairs. They emerged into another narrow hallway, with three rooms leading off from the left, a bathroom at the end and two further rooms leading off from the right. They passed the first door on the right. Buzan looked in and saw a kitchen. On the floor he noticed empty pizza boxes and beer cans. *And an empty bottle of chardonnay for the lady.* Chuck stretched out his arm as they approached the second door on right, immediately after the kitchen. Detective Constable Anneka Carlson stepped in first and saw in front of her Valerie Thomas and Christopher Woods. Both were sitting on a brown suede sofa. She approached them, Detective Constable Buzan following slightly behind her.

Valerie stood up first and started to speak before Carlson or Buzan had the chance to introduce themselves.

'Detectives, I really don't know how we can help you. We have already gone over everything we know about the events of Friday night. To be quite honest, I would rather just try to get on with life and forget about the whole thing.'

Valerie felt her confidence returning.

Detective Constable Buzan ignored the tone in her voice. 'Well, Ms Thomas,' he said, 'I'm afraid that that is not going to be possible just yet.'

Quite the little lawyer, thought Detective Constable Carlson as she studied Valerie's face.

'Now please, take a seat and we will tell you why we are here.'

Valerie looked to her male friends for support. Neither of them said anything. She sat down again. Anneka had learnt early into her policing career that there was a clever and subtle psychology behind choosing to remain standing. It was much like the dog mentality. The submissive member must roll over. All three students were now sitting and Detective Constable Carlson and Detective Constable Buzan were standing. That was much better.

'Valerie,' said Carlson, 'I am Detective Constable Anneka Carlson, and this is my partner Detective Constable Buzan. We work with the forensic response unit. We are involved in the investigation that is looking into the death of the victim you so tragically found late on Friday night.'

Good start, partner, Fuz thought. The girl looked more relaxed already.

'We have here in our hands the reports you gave to our uniformed colleagues shortly after you reported the discovery of the victim in Saline Park. I want to thank you firstly for calling the emergency services when you found the body.'

'Anybody would do the same,' said Christopher Woods.

Detective Constable Anneka Carlson studied him briefly, and continued, 'That's not completely true, I am afraid. You may be surprised that more than ninety per cent of witnesses to serious crime do not report anything. Although you are not strictly witnesses in the sense that you haven't witnessed a crime being committed, you are witnesses in that you found the body and thanks to the fact you didn't just run away, we have been able to determine that you were indeed the first individuals in the area where the body was left after it was placed there.'

Valerie shuddered.

'Do you know who the victim is?' she asked.

Detective Constable Buzan replied, 'No, we don't, unfortunately. Not at this stage.'

Valerie looked at Detective Constable Carlson.

'Do you know who the killer is?'

Detective Constable Carlson considered her answer carefully. 'Let's just say that we are pursuing all leads but we have not established the killer's identity as yet.'

Good answer, thought Buzan. He spoke up.

'Our visit here will be brief. We have come to let you know that our forensic scientists have been able to confirm everything that you reported to the officers on Friday night.'

He signalled to the witness statements in his hands.

'That's correct,' said Detective Constable Carlson. 'Thanks to your quick 999 call on Friday night and of course the fact that you remained at the scene until officers arrived, forensics have been able to determine by examining your footwear that you were simply passers-by to the crime.'

'How did they do that?' said Christopher Woods.

'It's a lengthy procedure that would take a while to explain,' replied Detective Constable Buzan. 'And I'm sure you understand that we need to use that time to continue solving this case. Suffice it to say, if you really want to know more about forensic science in this regard, I would suggest you Google "trainer tracking".'

There was a moment of silence as the group digested his words.

Chuck Adams spoke up.

'Hey, speaking of trainers, when are you guys going to return *ours* to us?'

Valerie rolled her eyes in frustration. Anneka reached into her pocket and pulled out one of her cards and a pen. She wrote down a phone number on the back and passed the card to Chuck.

'I suggest you call this number and ask for Julia Amos – she is one of our forensic scientists. She has your trainers.'

Detective Constable Buzan picked up on Anneka's tongue-in-cheek inflection when she said the words 'your trainers'.

'In the meantime,' she continued, 'if there's anything you want to speak to us about or clarify, please don't hesitate to give either of us a call. You can find our numbers on the front of our cards.' She took out two more of her cards and passed them to Christopher and Valerie. She then directed her gaze at Valerie and said, 'Valerie, you said earlier that you wanted to simply forget what has happened. Whilst I understand that, it may not be that easy. Sometimes people that make the kind of discovery that you did think they are OK and feel fine, but later on you may feel the need to speak to someone about what happened.'

Valerie returned her gaze.

'You mean like post-traumatic stress disorder?'

'Something like that, yes. Some people find that their views of the world radically change following such experiences. If you do feel the need to speak to anybody on an impartial basis, please call our main desk and someone will be able to help you. That goes for all of you,' she added, looking at each one individually.

'Well,' started Detective Constable Buzan, 'I think that we are done here.' As they established before they arrived at the student's house, their visit was intended to allow them to primarily see the students themselves and they always suspected that their visit would be quick. Uniformed officers had already taken statements.

They turned to let themselves out.

Carlson paused and looked back into the room, adding, 'And in future, when you are walking home, try to stick to well-lit public areas. And remember, if you are ever alone, always call a cab and let each other know where you are.'

The three students smiled in turn, each indicating that the message had been received. Carlson led the way back down the stairs and out through the front door.

Once back in the car, Detective Constable Buzan started the engine and pulled out of Upton Road, stopping again in a layby a few minutes' drive away so that the students wouldn't be able to see them.

'So, what did you think?' asked Carlson.

'As I said before, it was just formality and I didn't pick up on anything else. How about you?' Buzan answered.

'The same as you, basically: nothing suspicious, just formality. Why did you stop the car here?'

'Because', said Buzan, taking his mobile from out of his jacket pocket, 'I want to put a call through to the missing kids database. It's an automated system and because I was in the network earlier they have texted me through a pin, which means I can log in, enter the search fields and hopefully find something pertinent.'

Anneka did not speak but watched her partner as he dialled through. She heard an automated voice coming from his mobile and watched as he typed his responses, working his way through various menus. When he had reached the menu that asked him to enter the specific search terms he wanted to hone in on, he found himself struggling.

Anneka watched his growing frustration and offered her help.

'Start with approximate age and gender.'

He studied the basic search criteria and entered the responses on his keyboard: *'Gender?'* Male. *'Age or age range?'* 11-13. *'Missing since?'* He showed the menu to Detective Constable Carlson and the words popped up again. *'Missing since?'* This time an egg-timer indicating automatic log-out if he didn't reply within the next thirty seconds flashed up.

'Enter Sunday 2 October,' suggested Detective Constable Carlson, 'to cover the last week.'

He did as she recommended. The egg-timer icon reappeared, this time taking the full screen of his mobile, with the message 'please wait' flashing underneath.

They waited for at least a minute as his mobile download speed tried to catch up with the server. Eventually a new menu popped onto his screen. *'Search Term Results Found: 2: Click Here.'* Both Anneka and Buzan looked at one another before returning their gaze to the screen. Detective Constable Buzan tapped on the 'click here' instruction and two entries appeared.

The first was easy to dismiss as it detailed the reported

disappearance of a fifteen-year-old male who had gone missing from Bournemouth more than a week ago. The age was wrong. This meant that the system had included this individual's details as they had been the most recent entered before the second search results. *That's good*, Anneka found herself thinking. *At least there aren't any more missing kids out there reported in the last couple of weeks.*

With that, Buzan moved the keystroke function on to the second result found. This looked much more promising. It provided the details of a missing eleven-year-old male, who had disappeared from Halifax, in West Yorkshire. Before Buzan had had the chance to ask Detective Constable Carlson to calculate the distance, she had already pulled out her own mobile and was connected to Google maps.

'That's a distance of twenty-five miles from here, give or take a couple either side, depending on which route you take,' she said, her voice less sombre than previously. 'Can you see more information about the recorded disappearance?' she asked Detective Constable Buzan.

'Wait a second, I'm getting to that part now,' he replied.

The time seemed to drag as the page loaded.

'Oh my God,' said Anneka, a shiver moving down her spine as the image of the missing child downloaded. 'That's our victim.'

She felt a knot in her throat as a sense of both loathing and dread pulsed through her body.

Buzan felt the same sensations but continued to study the screen in front of him.

'Name: Stephen Sanderson.
Age: Eleven.
Eye colour: Brown.

Hair colour: Dark brown.

Height: 5 feet, 2 inches.

Weight: 51 kilos.

Last seen: Monday, October 3rd.

'Additional information: *"Stephen Sanderson was last seen on an escorted day trip to the Royal Armouries, approximately sixteen miles from Halifax, where he has lived as a permanent resident of the Halifax Children's Home for the past twelve months. He was last seen by a carer from the home. He disappeared at approximately 2.15 p.m. West Yorkshire Police are treating his disappearance as suspicious and urge anybody with information to come forward. Please contact Detective Chief Inspector Jane Theodorou on specialist police number 212 765 489 with any information."'*

The information sat on the screen motionless in front of both Buzan and Carlson. *They had found their victim's name.*

'Can you take a screen shot of this page and send it to all?' asked Anneka hurriedly.

'I can,' confirmed Detective Constable Buzan. 'I just have to be careful on here to enter all the names from my address book. This phone doesn't auto-save from the last emails.'

'OK,' said Anneka. 'I'll say the names and you enter them so we can both check if we have missed anyone. Put in Roberts.'

Buzan typed R and Detective Inspector James Roberts appeared first. He clicked select.

'Put in Dr Laos.'

He did so as Detective Constable Carlson spoke.

'Detective Chief Inspector Morti,' she continued. 'You and

113

I obviously. The generic forensics address, which will make sure that Detective Inspector Stubs and Julia Amos and their teams get the same information at the same time.'

'You forgot someone,' said Detective Constable Buzan after he had entered the names and addresses Anneka had been reading off from her mental checklist.

'Who?' she replied, none the wiser.

'Trevor Stephenson, the forensic psychologist chap,' confirmed Detective Constable Buzan.

He turned his gaze back to the screen in front of him, added Stephenson and clicked 'send'. He looked up and faced Detective Constable Carlson, and they held one another's stare for some time. They both knew that although they had made a positive identification on their victim, there was still a long way to go before they could conclude this case. Identification of the victim meant that somebody's life was soon going to change forever. A victim had a family, a victim had friends. *Even if that family was a state institution*, Anneka thought. Many lives would change. As such thoughts crossed both their minds, Anneka Carlson's mobile phone rang. It was Detective Inspector Roberts. *He was certainly quick not to waste any time.*

'Anneka, good work, please let Detective Constable Buzan know how grateful we are for the identification.'

His voice was punctuated and he spoke loudly.

'I'm with Dr Laos. She has, in the absence of any current next of kin or official guardian, provisionally identified the victim as Stephen Sanderson. We will take the case from here until further notice. Morti wants us all back at the station for a meeting at 3 p.m. sharp. We are on our way to a chemist, who we hope can help us with the hydrogen peroxide and benzodiazepine leads, so we will see you both at three.'

With that he ended the call.

Buzan smiled at Anneka. He had heard the detective inspector loud and clear.

Chapter Ten

Sunday 9 October, 12.45 p.m.,
Oldham, Greater Manchester

Detective Inspector Roberts had been more than happy to continue to let Dr Laos drive her car for the duration of their afternoon appointments. He sat comfortably in the passenger seat, occasionally playing with the automatic CD selector. He found her music interesting. In his own car, he was lucky to get the radio's auto-scan function to work. His aerial had been partially snapped off by a drive-in car wash several years back and he had tried fixing it himself with the help of some sellotape and an old metallic coat hanger. It had been a standing joke among his colleagues ever since.

Now, as the two drove onto the A62 across the nine-and-a-half mile distance from Manchester's inner city to the outlying suburb of Oldham where they were due to meet the chemist that Karen had spoken about previously, Detective Inspector Roberts reclined back in the passenger seat, listening to The Cure's 'Charlotte Sometimes'.

'So,' he began, 'tell me about this chemist we are about to meet.'

Karen lowered the volume on her stereo.

'Her name is Joan Jackson. I've known her since I was a child – she's a friend of my mother's. But, more to the point, she is an excellent industrial chemist who I have worked with professionally on several cases.'

'A friend of your mother's?' came Roberts' obvious question, one which Karen would have rather avoided as it might lead to other, more uncomfortable topics.

Nonetheless, she had started trusting him and decided to indulge his curiosity.

'Yes, she was my mother's best friend throughout her marriage to my father. I practically grew up considering her an aunt and her children were more like siblings than my own brother.'

The words crossed her mind, along with other more unsettling thoughts. *I haven't spoken to my own brother in years. The occasional Christmas card here and there and little else.*

Roberts saw that Karen was deep in thought and decided to change the subject back to one more related to the case.

'So why is an industrial chemist working as a high-street pharmacist?'

His question was certainly pertinent.

'It was her choice,' replied Karen. 'She's close to retirement age and decided to move from the pressures of working for the massive pharmaceutical industry about four years ago. She trained in medicinal chemistry in London back in the 1960s. She moved up to Manchester after she completed her PhD thesis on the metabolism of chemical structures in the human body.'

She checked Detective Inspector Roberts' face to ascertain whether he was still with her. He was. *He would have to be, given all he has seen,* she found herself thinking.

'So that's why you knew she would be the perfect person to tell us all about benzodiazepines and hydrogen peroxide?' asked Roberts.

'Exactly,' replied Karen. 'She has more expertise in her head than a hundred textbooks. She has worked in pharmaceuticals, manufacturing and organic chemistry. She is one of the most celebrated chemists of her era.'

Strange that she's now working in a pharmacy in Oldham, thought Detective Inspector Roberts. Then again, could he see himself easily retiring in a few years' time? *Not a chance – they would have to kill me first.*

Karen pulled her car into a busy shopping street. Across the road a green pharmacy sign flashed in dull neon lights. The name 'Jackson's Pharmacy' was visible beneath the canopy overhanging the shop's entrance. Detective Inspector Roberts got out of the car first, scanning the street as he waited for Karen to lock the doors. He knew the suburbs of Greater Manchester like a map etched indelibly into his mind but it had been a while since he had been in this particular area.

The traffic was heavy for a Sunday, the street full of puddles and potholes from the recent bad weather. The sky was hazy and threatened further rain. They crossed the street, Karen two steps ahead of her partner. As she opened the door to the pharmacy, a small woman of no more than five foot four smiled at her from across the counter. A few customers were busy checking beauty products in the aisles. Joan Jackson looked her age, and wore a small pair of spectacles. Detective Inspector Roberts studied her hands as they approached her counter; she had the hands of someone that had worked hard for many years, a callus or two the evidence of a long career.

She greeted Dr Laos first, coming out from behind her desk and embracing her with the affection and warmth that one would expect of a family member.

'Karen,' she said, 'it has been too long. How are you, my love?'

Her London accent remained, despite the number of years she had lived in the north.

'I'm fine, thank you, Joan,' replied Karen, displaying a level of warmth and reciprocal affection that Roberts had until now not seen.

'Let me introduce you to Detective Inspector James Roberts,' she said, her left arm extended to tell the inspector to join in the conversation.

'How do you do, Inspector?' asked Joan, her hand open in greeting.

Detective Inspector Roberts shook her hand and replied, 'Very well, thank you. I'm pleased to meet you. I wish it was under different circumstances.'

His words were low in tone. Joan Jackson understood his meaning.

'Yes, Karen has told me why you are here. Please, come with me. We can sit in privacy out the back. It's nothing grand but it will suffice.'

As she scuttled off, her guests in tow, she indicated to a shop assistant that she would be gone for ten minutes.

They entered a small storage room with just an under-sized desk and one chair. Joan sat. Dr Laos and Detective Inspector James Roberts remained standing.

'So, Karen tells me that you would like to know more about hydrogen peroxide and benzodiazepines, particularly the brand we call clonazepam?'

She spoke in Detective Inspector Roberts' direction.

119

'Yes, please,' he replied. 'We are dealing with a murder case at present.' He looked at Karen. 'Dr Laos has been able to determine that the victim has both external and internal indications of hydrogen peroxide. It is also evident that the victim had been drugged with clonazepam prior to death. Specifically, we would like to know where our killer may have got his hands on these substances.'

Joan Jackson considered his question before responding.

'To be honest with you, Inspector, the killer could have obtained both materials from practically anywhere.' She looked solemn. 'I don't think you will have much luck in tracing the source of the clonazepam.' 'I say that for several reasons. Primarily, unless you have the name or potential name of your killer there would be no point in checking prescriptions that have been issued. Even if you did know the name of your killer, he or she could have cashed in their prescription anywhere in the country, or indeed on any of the *legal* internet pharmacies now available. That, quite simply put, would be a massive search.'

Detective Inspector Roberts contemplated her words.

'Well, the profile we seem to be looking at for the killer does not seem to fit someone who is themselves a user of this medication. I say that because—'

He was cut off mid-sentence by Joan Jackson.

'Because you don't think that you are looking for someone who has psychological issues that would require medication. You are looking for somebody that is using this substance purely as a means to an end in his killings?'

She was spot on. Detective Inspector Roberts, somewhat taken aback, looked over at Karen. She intervened.

'Yes, Joan, you're right. We are looking at a profile of some-body with a psychopathic personality, not a mental illness.'

Joan flicked her gaze between Karen and Detective Inspector Roberts.

'In that case, I would hope for your sake that this killer is not himself taking the medication.'

'Why do you say that?' asked Roberts.

'Because, Inspector, psychopathic personalities also very frequently have addictive tendencies. They may use drugs such as benzodiazepines in order to placate their own sense of worthlessness. Alcohol may be abused in the same way.'

She saw the surprised look in Detective Inspector Roberts' face.

'Inspector, I am no psychologist but I have worked with these medications for a long time, in research and practice. I have picked up a fair bit over the years.'

'Of course you have. I'm sorry, Dr Jackson, please continue,' he said somewhat sheepishly, recalling at the same time that this lady had a PhD.

'In that case, if you are following the assumption that your killer has a psychopathic personality, you can also be damn sure that he will have gone to great lengths to hide his tracks. As the police you have at your disposal the means of checking all recent purchases across the country of clonazepam, even if he had purchased them online, without a prescription, from one of the many *illegal* pharmacies that have sprung up in this wonderful age of the internet, using fake IP addresses, often shipping from the Indian sub-continent.'

Detective Inspector Roberts thought about the profile he was looking at for this killer.

'That wouldn't fit either,' he said. 'We have determined that this is a killer that values, even requires, extreme privacy.'

Karen intervened.

'We have also determined, Joan, that the victim disappeared from his last known location last Monday. Blood work indicates that he was administered with clonazepam, certainly from Thursday 6 October, for a period of approximately twenty-four hours and likely before, following his disappearance. Of course, the drug's half-life doesn't allow for us to trace the substance any further back than Thursday. Blood work has also determined from the elimination half-life of the drug that the victim received a total of sixteen milligrams in that time frame.'

'Wow,' said Joan. 'That is a hell of a dose. I have only seen that level of benzodiazepine use once in my career and that was years ago when I interned in a psychiatric ward. A patient in the manic phase of bipolar disorder required the same level in order to simply get some sleep.'

Years ago. Joan's words stayed in Detective Inspector Roberts' mind. He thumped the desk, startling both Dr Laos and Joan Jackson.

'That's it!' he exclaimed. 'Tell me, please, how long would someone be able to store clonazepam before it expired?'

'Well,' said Joan, 'that is an excellent question. Contrary to popular belief, medication does not expire in the same manner as the drug companies would like us to think.'

'So you are saying that our killer could be hanging on to old stores of this drug?' asked James, his pulse beating faster with anticipation.

'Indeed I am, Inspector. Have you ever reached for a box of paracetamol with a splitting headache only to find they had expired?'

'Yes, I have.'

'And what did you do when you saw the pills were past their expiration date?'

'I took them anyway,' replied Roberts.

'Exactly,' said Joan. 'And, as you're here in the room with us, apparently healthy, I assume that they didn't make you sick?'

'No, they took the damn headache away.'

'Well,' said Joan, 'Karen has brought you to me for a reason. She knows that I studied the efficacy of expired medications as a part of my PhD thesis.'

Karen looked slightly pleased with herself.

'And what did you find?' asked Roberts.

'Something that the drug company paying for my PhD wished that I hadn't,' said Joan. 'Specifically, let's just say that aspects of my thesis were excluded from final publica tion. They told me to look elsewhere.' She had the look of someone whose thoughts were anchored heavily in the past as she spoke. 'I determined that the expiration date on a drug does stand for something, but probably not what you think it does. Since a law was passed 1979, drug manufacturers are required to stamp an expiration date on their products. This is the date at which the manufacturer can still guarantee the full potency and safety of the drug. Before that time, not all medication stated the drug's expiry date.

'Most of what is known about drug expiration dates comes from various scientific studies conducted by a range of bodies, including the Food and Drug Administration in the United States at, I add, the request of the military. It was concerned with its own large and expensive stockpile of drugs and found itself facing the possibility of tossing them out and replacing the drugs every few years. What they found from the study is that over ninety per cent of more than one hundred drugs, both prescription and over-the-counter, were perfectly good to use even thirty years after the expiration date. That study included and references clonazepam.'

'I can see why the pharmaceutical company that sponsored your PhD would have wanted that excluded from your research back then,' said Detective Inspector Roberts.

Karen nodded her agreement as Joan continued.

'So the expiration date stated these days on many medications doesn't really indicate a point at which the medication is no longer effective or has become unsafe to use. Medical authorities state expired drugs are safe to take, even those that expired years ago. A rare exception to this may be tetracycline, but the report on this is controversial among researchers. It's true that the effectiveness of a drug may decrease over time, but much of the original potency still remains even after two decades following the expiration date. Excluding nitroglycerin, insulin and liquid antibiotics, most medications are as long lasting as the ones tested by the military. Placing a medication in a cool place, such as a refrigerator, will help a drug remain potent for many years.'

Detective Inspector Roberts made a note in his pad as she spoke: *Refrigerators help maintain potency.*

'Is the expiration date a marketing ploy by drug manufacturers, to keep you restocking your medicine cabinet and their pockets regularly?' asked Karen.

Joan contemplated her question.

'You can look at it that way. Or you can also look at it this way: the expiration dates are very conservative to ensure you get everything you paid for. And, really, if a drug manufacturer had to do expiration-date testing for longer periods, it would slow their ability to bring you new and improved formulations.'

'Either way,' interjected Roberts, 'you have provided us

124

with some very valuable information, for which we are very grateful.'

'You're both more than welcome,' said Joan, adding, 'I hope it goes some way in helping you locate your antagonist.'

'It certainly saves us time,' said Karen, 'meaning that we don't have to search an entire national database of prescriptions for clonazepam.'

'I believe that you also wanted to ask me about hydrogen peroxide?' asked Joan Jackson, summoning both Roberts and Karen to re-engage in their questions. 'Tell me what you have found so far with regard to the killer's use of hydrogen peroxide.'

'Well,' began Karen, 'I have been able to ascertain that the killer is using hydrogen peroxide in order to firstly assist with what appears to be removing aspects of the victim's body parts, namely superficial skin removals. I was also able to determine that the hydrogen peroxide found in our victim is of the same strength and age found in a victim from a case that both I and Detective Inspector Roberts worked on together six years ago.'

'Peroxide homicide,' said Joan, deep in recall. 'I remember the case. I also remember the media had a field day with it.' She looked at Karen. 'I remember too how you suffered on that case.'

Karen was surprised at her friend's words but continued nonetheless. 'Yes, it would seem that we are dealing with the same killer. So, yes, you are right, there is an element of this whole thing that feels personal, not only for me, but I think for my partner in all this, Detective Inspector Roberts.'

He looked up, the understanding and agreement shining from his eyes.

'The fact that you have been able to determine that the

hydrogen peroxide found in both of your victims is of the same source tells me one thing of which there can be no doubt,' said Joan.

Her audience waited for her to continue. She adjusted her chair slightly, making herself more comfortable and looked up at Dr Laos and the inspector, both of whom were still standing.

'It tells me that the killer you are looking for has to be storing his supply of hydrogen peroxide in a dark place. If exposed to light, H_2O_2 runs the risk of deteriorating into H_2O, in other words, water. Hydrogen peroxide can be kept indefinitely, under the correct conditions. Such conditions would not only include a dark place, but one which is also cool.' She thought as she spoke. 'A suitable and easily obtainable vessel for such storage would include plastic drums, which you could buy from any garden centre or DIY facility.'

She addressed her next question to Karen.

'Tell me, Karen, when you analyzed the H_2O_2 compound on your most recent victim, did you find that the hydrogen peroxide contained trace elements of an aqueous solution of sulphuric acid or acidic ammonium bisulphate?'

Karen thought for ten seconds before responding.

'Yes, I did. I ran the evidence in the Gaseous Vapour Decontamination and Maturity Detector and found the substance to be at least fifteen years old and ammonium bisulphate was detected. Why do you ask? What does it mean?'

'It means, Karen, that the hydrogen peroxide you are seeking was certainly produced before fifteen years ago and, at best guess, I would say before twenty years. In the last two decades hydrogen peroxide has been manufactured using a slightly different method, one which replaces ammonium bisulphate with the hydrolysis of the peroxodisulphate.'

'That means,' said Detective Inspector Roberts, 'that not only is the killer using old supplies of clonazepam but he is also using old supplies of hydrogen peroxide. The forensic psychologist was right. He would require a high degree of privacy in order to store these materials.'

Karen looked up. Joan saw her deflated look. She recognized it well.

'Don't worry, Karen, there is no reason you would have picked up on that, which is why I assume you sought my services.'

There was no question in her voice and it made Karen feel better.

'How long could the killer store his supply of hydrogen peroxide for?' asked Detective Inspector Roberts, adding, 'Indefinitely?'

Dr Jackson thought briefly.

'Hydrogen peroxide decomposes, or disproportionates exothermically into water and oxygen gas spontaneously. Therefore, as long as the killer avoids exposing his stash to high temperatures, there is no reason why he could not store his stockpile for very many years to come.' She addressed Karen. 'Were you able to determine the strength of the H_2O_2 under analysis?'

'Yes, I was,' she replied. 'I determined that the concentration was at a minimum level of thirty-five per cent. Why do you ask?'

'Just to further clarify my last statement. You see, a six per cent strength of hydrogen peroxide decomposes at one volume per twenty volumes of oxygen. This has serious implications for the necessity behind the safe storage of the substance. The liberation of oxygen and energy in the decomposition has dangerous side effects. Spilling high concentrations of hydrogen peroxide on a flammable substance can cause an immediate fire, which is further fuelled by the oxygen released by the decomposing hydrogen peroxide.'

'So,' said Detective Inspector Roberts, 'our killer treasures and protects his stash. He is careful and takes very few risks. That also fits the profile of a trophy killer.'

Karen checked her own thoughts and found that she agreed with what Detective Inspector Roberts had said.

Detective Inspector Roberts turned his next question to Dr Jackson.

'Can you tell us which companies were producing hydrogen peroxide using ammonium bisulphate approximately twenty years ago?'

Joan Jackson needed no time to think about her response.

'Yes, I can,' she said. 'In this region of the United Kingdom at the time there were only two manufacturers and only three in the entire country. One was located in Hastings, on the south coast. The other two, in this region, were operating out of Leeds and Greater Manchester respectively. The laboratory in Leeds was called Leeds Chemical and Analytical Services. The other was located right here in Oldham. It went by the name of Jackson and Lawrence Industrial Chemical Services.'

Both Detective Inspector Roberts and Dr Laos opened their mouths in surprise.

'I suppose it would be a foolish question to ask,' said Roberts, 'but were you the Jackson in the company name?'

'Yes, I was. And Lawrence was my old partner, Joel Lawrence. He died a long time ago now. Modesty aside, Inspector, we operated one of the most successful manufacturing plants of chemical compounds ever to have been seen in this country. But that all changed when Lawrence passed away.'

Karen looked both surprised and hurt. Joan saw the look on her face.

'Karen, I am sure you want to ask me why I never mentioned this before. It just didn't seem necessary. Your mother and I met in a social setting and became best friends as a result. She never asked me about the intricacies of my work so I never told her that I was in fact, until four years ago, the managing director of Jackson and Lawrence. Therefore you were not to know that either.'

'You were there until four years ago?' asked Detective Inspector Roberts, his question rhetorical as he continued. 'But I have never heard of this company before and I know this area like the back of my hand.'

He sounded exasperated.

'No, Inspector, you wouldn't have. After Joel died nineteen years ago, the company changed names but I continued as a managing director and a consultant until what was left of the organization finally went into liquidation four years ago. Thanks to multinational drug companies, I am all that is left of that era.'

As she said the word 'I', she placed her hands across her chest. *That certainly explains why she now runs a pharmacy in a washed-out part of Oldham,* thought Detective Inspector Roberts, feeling sad for the elderly woman who had achieved and lost so much in her life. He moved on to his next question.

'Is there any way that you could access your records pertaining to any private customers that might have purchased large quantities of hydrogen peroxide from your company approximately twenty years ago?'

Dr Jackson looked thoughtful.

'Yes, of course I can, Inspector. I kept records of every single transaction made back then.'

She smiled, adding, 'I was also chief accountant.' *That didn't save me from the sharks,* she added in her head.

She stood up from behind her desk and moved to some large and dusty box files that sat on shelves in the corner of the room. She returned after a few moments with two folders of paper records stored neatly in transparent sleeves. She opened the first box file and flicked open a page entitled 'Personal Customer Accounts: 1980–1998'.

'This,' she said, 'contains eighteen years of transactions. These are records we kept for cash customers only. If anybody made frequent purchases of hydrogen peroxide and paid by cash in this time-frame, I will have a record of it here.' She sounded very sure of herself. 'This,' she continued, riffling through papers, 'is very interesting.'

Detective Inspector Roberts looked at Karen and she returned his probing glance. They stayed quiet and let Dr Jackson continue.

'The customer code and number on this receipt.'

She pulled out a partly yellow-stained A5-sized piece of paper.

'PCW81 tells me that a personal cash account was opened in 1981. Here.'

She indicated with a swollen forefinger, as her fingernail moved down and across the piece of paper.

'This customer, whose name was William McDonald, purchased a 250 litre plastic drum containing just under 205,000 millilitres of hydrogen peroxide in February 1981.' She chuckled to herself. 'My, how prices have changed. In 1981 the cost for such a purchase was £4 per litre.' She did a quick calculation. 'Nowadays the same amount of hydrogen peroxide at the same food-grade strength would cost you £30.'

'That means,' added Karen, 'that this William McDonald paid approximately £820 in 1981, which was a hell of a lot of money back then.'

Detective Inspector Roberts concurred. 'Indeed it was. I remember paying ten pence for a loaf of bread, which seemed then like it would break the bank.'

Joan Jackson continued moving her finger up and down the A5 paper in front of her, before filing it back into the plastic sleeve from which she had removed it and opening another part of the folder.

'This customer's number reappears again in March 1982.' She turned her gaze to Detective Inspector Roberts. 'At that time he again purchased a 205 litre plastic drum containing just less than 205,000 millilitres of hydrogen peroxide.'

'Is there any chance that you remember this buyer?' asked Detective Inspector Roberts hopefully. 'Or that you have an address for him?'

'I'm afraid not, Detective, I wasn't involved in the actual selling of our products. However . . .'

She again anchored her mind back to the past. 'I do recall finding it unusual when going through the accounts for someone to buy such large quantities now that I think of it, given that the buyer was not a pharmaceutical partner.'

'Did he buy any more?' asked Karen.

Joan flicked through some further pages before closing the folder and opening the next. After what seemed like an eternity, she replied.

'Yes, my dear, he did. Right here.'

She pointed down at another page: this time the year read 1983. The month was January. Roberts looked at the page. The same customer code: PCW81. The same purchase: 205 litre plastic drum with just under 205,000 millilitres of hydrogen peroxide.

'Dr Jackson, I hate to ask, but did it not seem relevant six years ago to let the police know that you had records of these purchases when you heard the media refer to the previous case with the words *"peroxide homicide"*?'

She contemplated the inspector's words. 'Inspector,' she said, 'six years ago I was still working for my disintegrating company. I didn't even look at these records until you asked me to today. Had I recalled any part of them, believe me, I would most certainly have come forward to the police.'

Detective Inspector Roberts believed her.

'Thank you, Dr Jackson. Can we please take a copy of those three invoices with us? I'm sure you'll appreciate that we need to run some checks on that customer's name.'

Dr Jackson was quick to reply.

'If you will give me a few minutes, I will make some copies of these on the fax machine I have out the back.'

She scuttled off in the opposite direction.

'I can see why you think so fondly of her,' Detective Inspector Roberts said to Karen as they waited for her to return.

'Yes.' Karen found herself agreeing. 'There just seems to be a lot about her life that I always took for granted and assumed I knew. Now I find out I knew only the basics.'

'Don't be so hard on yourself, Karen,' replied Detective Inspector Roberts. 'We all have our secrets, and hers seem innocent enough.'

Karen concurred but said nothing as she thought about her past, her childhood and everything that was going on currently.

Chapter Eleven

Sunday 9 October, 2 p.m.

He had been careful on his most recent trip to stick to quiet country lanes rather than main roads. It increased his journey times but also his safety and efficiency. The car that he drove, although infrequently, had belonged to his father as a 'collector's piece'. His father had rarely driven it, preferring instead to use his main Vauxhall Estate. *He had been pleased to burn that piece of shit when he had got his father out of his way.*

He liked to think of his own tastes as much more refined and therefore on special occasions would slowly uncover his late father's 1976 Ford Elite, replete with a fully working V8 engine of 5.8 litres, from beneath the tarpaulin under which it was safely stored in the main garage of the house. Today he stood admiring the car, reflecting upon his recent work.

The garage, built off the main building of the house, was twelve metres long and four in width. Like the rest of the house, it too was in urgent need of repair, but it hadn't fallen down in all these years and it was very unlikely that it would during his lifetime. He had no desires towards repairing the house. It was simply his shell and he concentrated his efforts on his own self-improvement.

He had wanted to tell his father just how stupid he had thought him to be to keep this beauty of a machine under wraps. The cloth bench seats were in perfect condition and the green metallic glow paint a real crowning achievement, second only in his mind to the black glass paint he had himself applied to the windows. It provided the perfect cover for his needs. Nobody could see in but he had a full and unobstructed view out. Much like the rest of his life. He retained complete control at every opportunity.

It had been almost a week since he had last ventured out from the privacy and protection of his house. The day had been full of rain and the sky black and ominous. He had planned a day where he knew he would find his next prop. He had planned his journey with as much skill and attention as he felt appropriate, a level equalled only by the attention he placed on the work he was completing.

The fifteen-mile trip would have been quicker had he taken the M62 for several miles and then joined the A629, but that would have left him fully exposed and would have defeated the purpose of his trip. He had sworn to Abeona that he would return with a gift to honour her name. In return she had endowed him with strength. Best of all, he had got to keep his trophies.

He had left his house mid-morning and snaked his way through the countryside, the tools he would need placed carefully on the back seat behind where he sat. He had his home-crushed clonazepam in a small sandwich bag, which he concealed in his jacket pocket. He figured that two pills of two-milligram strength would take effect within a maximum of thirty minutes on a naïve victim.

Just the start he needed to get the process underway. He had passed through villages such as Littleborough and Ripponden, then sneaked through the outskirts of Leeds towards his destination, the Royal Armouries.

He knew that he would be spotted as the odd one out in an attraction park full of mums, dads, grandparents and children. A lone male, pulling into the car park, he would certainly be registered by the security CCTV cameras. Bearing these thoughts in mind, he had taken his time as all good hunters did.

Pulling up alongside a disused factory not far from the Royal Armouries, he had tucked his vehicle out of sight. He opened the back left door of the car and removed his backpack. The first thing he knew he would need was a diversion, something to attract the prop that he would select. To this end, he kitted himself up like a soldier, a small pellet gun tucked into his belt strap. A gun would surely do the trick at an attraction such as an armoury.

Inside his backpack he had placed only the essentials. A gag in case his prop started to scream, a one-and-a-half-metre length of rope to tie his hands. The last thing he wanted was a child thrashing its way around the back of his car. He placed too much value on the quality of the seats to risk them being damaged. With this in mind he had also covered the back seats with a blanket. *Unsightly but necessary*, he had thought to himself.

He had packed some cans of soft drinks; a carrot on a stick that had worked for him in the past. He had checked his watch and seen the time approaching one in the afternoon, then pulled out his ordnance survey map of the locality. The Royal Armouries was just less than a mile from his present location. If he headed in a northerly direction at a fast pace across the field ahead of him, he could skirt into the vicinity in just under ten minutes.

He smiled to himself as he recollected how his day had panned out. Everything had gone so smoothly, his plans well adhered to. He hadn't got too close to the main hub of activity at the armouries, just close enough to single out the first suitable prop he had seen. When safely inside the perimeter, he had taken refuge from the rain beneath an abandoned recreation of a World War II look-out post. *A cheap khaki imitation to keep the gullible visitors entertained,* he had thought. It had served his plans well, however.

He had checked his watch, the time now close to 1.20. He made himself as comfortable as he could and waited for 40 minutes. It was then, at 2 p.m., that he had seen his prop approach. A lone male not old enough to be considered an adult, but still young enough to pass as a child. *Abeona would be pleased.*

He ducked out from under the look-out post, pretended not to notice the boy, then removed his pellet gun and started to play the role of a soldier keeping watch.

From the corner of his eye he saw his young prop peeing against a bush. The young male's curiosity grew as he saw the soldier bent over the look-out post, aiming his gun into the field nearby.

'Hey, mister!' the child called as he walked closer. 'What are you looking at?'

Playing the part of an actor in the recreation, he had turned his gaze in the young male's direction. He had thought carefully about how he would reply.

'Hey, fella, don't you know it's rude to interrupt a soldier when he's on duty?'

The young boy's face had fallen.

'However,' he had started, needing to keep the kid entertained, 'you look like a strong boy.'

The kid had grinned. His diversion had worked. *Reel him in, capture his interest, scold him, and then bring him back.* It was a psychological trick he figured would make the kid feel safe. It had worked perfectly.

'I'm keeping lookout for the enemy,' he had said, his voice emotionless.

The kid had obviously assumed that this guy was just one of the many actors he had met during the day so far and decided to play along.

'Can I help you?' he had asked the soldier.

The soldier had looked hesitant at first but eventually replied with the answer the boy was hoping for.

'Sure you can, kid. I hope you're a good runner cos we have to cross that field there in less than ten minutes.'

The boy had looked a little wary.

'Maybe I should check with Miss Hitchens,' he had said to the soldier.

'Did Miss Hitchens pay for your ticket here today, kid?'

He had felt pleased with his acting skills.

'Yes, she did,' the prop had replied.

'In that case, wouldn't Miss Hitchens be upset if you didn't take advantage of all the activities she has paid for you to enjoy?'

The kid had thought for a short while, then grinned and replied, 'Where do we start and who are we looking for?'

Everything's going so well, the soldier had thought.

'Well, the enemy is hard to find, but I think he headed in that direction.'

He had pointed to where he knew his car was parked.

'And as you're playing along so well, why don't you have a

can of cola to drink on the way?'

He had pulled out from his backpack a can of coke before the kid had had chance to answer. He had been careful to open it for the kid, making sure he could slip the four milligrams of clonazepam into the can before he passed it to him. He had watched carefully as he took his first gulp.

'Come on, fella, we better make a start. Keep up with me, OK?'

The kid had grinned and they had set off across the field, pellet gun in his hand as they jogged, making sure he kept up the illusion of being a soldier on watch.

He had wanted the kid to tire out sooner rather than later so had made sure that the journey took slightly longer than it would have taken normally. They'd lapped the field twice and as they approached the abandoned factory on the far side, he had noticed that the kid was starting to take steps that were mismatched. The drug had started taking effect already.

'Hey, kid, keep up, we can take a rest there.'

He had pointed with his right hand at the shell of a factory.

'And,' he'd added, 'drink your cola, it's full of energy.'

The kid had done as he was told. They'd reached the factory, the kid unaware of the Ford Elite that was tucked out of sight. *The car that would ultimately take him on his last road trip ever.* They had stopped and the kid had been told to sit down. As he'd sat down he'd stumbled slightly.

'Hey, fella, looks like that little run has taken it out of you. Let's sit here for a few minutes before we carry on.'

He'd checked his watch and seen the time turn to 2.25 p.m. He knew that by now the kid would have been noticed as missing. He also knew that within the next few minutes the kid would be drowsy enough to bundle into his car.

As the next two minutes passed, he had watched the kid falling into a slumber and scooped him up, his hand around the kid's mouth to keep him quiet. The kid had realized that something was wrong and tried to resist. By then it was too late and he felt himself being thrown onto the back seat of a car. He had been quickly gagged and had his hands and feet tied together.

He let a further five minutes pass before starting the engine of the car. As the car purred its way across the same back lanes of the countryside he had driven along on the way, he had heard the kid gently snoring in the back seat. He had felt pleased with himself; had checked his watch, knowing that he would be home with his prop within the hour.

Chapter Twelve

Sunday 9 October, 3 p.m.,
Greater Manchester Police Headquarters

Detective Chief Inspector Philip Morti presided over the incident room like a referee at the centre of a boxing ring. He stood and reviewed his audience. Assembled in the seats in front of him, on time as he had demanded, were Detective Inspector Roberts, Dr Karen Laos, Detective Constable Anneka Carlson and Detective Constable Frank Buzan. Also assembled into the corner of the incident room were Detective Inspector Paula Stubs, forensic scientist Julia Amos and the psychologist Trevor Stephenson.

They hadn't been required, but they had, like the rest of the station, heard about the positive identification made on the victim and the equally interesting news that Detective Inspector Roberts and Dr Laos had a name from the chemist Dr Joan Jackson that may be of great interest to the investigation. Julia Amos had recently left a meeting with her team and also had some information to pass over to the detectives working the case.

Detective Chief Inspector Morti was dressed in his finest

suit, cufflinks and tie in place.

'So,' he said, 'we are into the second day of this investigation. You have all worked long hours and I am pleased with the efforts you have all made.' He paused, checking the faces of the crowd. 'However, there is much work still to follow.' He checked his watch, a heavy gold Rolex. 'I have invited the media to come in forty-five minutes' time.'

Karen looked at Roberts. He remained motionless.

'I have been speaking to Detective Chief Inspector Jane Theodorou from the West Yorkshire police force. She and her team have been to visit the staff and residents of the Halifax Children's Home. Needless to say, the boy's designated carer on the day, a Miss Hitchens, is distraught by the events that occurred last Monday.'

He directed his attention to Karen Laos.

'Dr Laos, the staff from Detective Chief Inspector Theodorou's team are sending a hairbrush and a toothbrush that belonged to Stephen Sanderson over to your staff at the mortuary as we speak so that we can acquire a one hundred per cent match on the victim. It is purely for confirmatory reasons, as you all know.'

'That,' said Karen in response, 'is a very quick procedure. I would expect my staff to send me an email within a few minutes of receiving the items.'

'Indeed,' replied Detective Chief Inspector Morti, his stare fixed on Karen. 'I would expect the items to be at your mortuary within the next half an hour. In the meantime, now that we can assume that we have a positive identification on the victim, the time is right for us to start speaking to the press. As we all know, they are in the position to be able to help us reach the general public, who, with the help of our staff, may be able to lead us to the killer.'

He looked over at Detective Inspector Roberts, his gaze telling the inspector that he wanted him to stand up. Roberts complied.

'James, please, for the benefit of everyone in the room, can you outline the findings that have arisen as a result of your and Dr Laos's visit to the chemist today?'

Roberts cleared his throat before beginning.

'Well, firstly, we had a very productive visit to an industrial chemist by the name of Dr Joan Jackson. We had visited her on the advice of Dr Laos, who felt, quite correctly I may add, that this lady would be able to help us trace hydrogen peroxide that was produced in the timeframe of between fifteen to twenty years ago, which was the approximate age attributed to the hydrogen peroxide found on both victims.'

He looked at Karen for confirmation. She raised an eye that told him he was correct.

'Dr Jackson was able to confirm that there is absolutely no reason why the killer has not been using an old storage he has of hydrogen peroxide. The same applies to the use of the benzodiazepines. Suffice it to say I found myself on the end of a very educational visit today.'

Detective Constable Anneka Carlson looked at him in a way that told him that she was curious to know more. 'Dr Jackson also informed us that for certain medications, including clonazepam, expiry dates have no bearing on the drug's potency or indeed ability to carry out their purpose, as long as they are stored in cool, dark and suitable conditions. It would seem that in certain cases drug expiry dates are there for the benefit of the pharmaceutical companies that produce them. The same applies to hydrogen peroxide.'

He turned to Trevor Stephenson.

'Trevor, the chemist we met today was very knowledgeable

in some unexpected ways. You told us that we should be looking at the profile of a killer who values above all his privacy?'

Trevor Stephenson, a fat, tall man, wheezed as he spoke.

'That is correct, Inspector. And from what you have just said, it would add further evidence to this theory. Storing these substances would require space and isolation.'

Detective Chief Inspector Morti looked like he had the weight of the world on his shoulders as he pushed Detective Inspector Roberts to continue.

'Inspector, please can you skip to the most important part?'

Roberts, looking slightly annoyed with his superior, continued. 'It turns out that until four years ago Dr Joan Jackson was the managing director of a pharmaceutical and research organization based in Oldham, called Jackson and Lawrence Industrial Chemical Services. The company changed names about nineteen years ago when Dr Jackson's partner Lawrence died, but she continued in the capacity of a specialist consultant and MD for the organization until four years ago when the company finally went bust. Dr Jackson now owns a small family pharmacy out in Oldham.'

Detective Inspector Roberts sensed that his colleagues each had questions they wanted to ask but nobody spoke, given Morti's insistence that things be hurried along. *The big cheese and the media,* he found himself thinking. He pushed the thought aside and continued.

'It turns out that Dr Jackson is also somewhat of an accomplished accountant, having managed the financial affairs of Jackson and Lawrence. She kept all records from the company and was able to locate for us an individual by the name of William McDonald who purchased three 205 litre plastic drums, each containing just less than 205,000 millilitres of hydrogen peroxide. He spread his purchases out over the years of 1981, 1982 and 1983. What makes this important to us is that there were only three producers in the UK of industrial- or food-grade strength H_2O_2 at the time Mr McDonald made his purchases, one being right here in Manchester.'

Detective Chief Inspector Morti interrupted, lifting his phone and calling the detectives manning the incident room phones a level below.

'I want a search on the name of William McDonald,' he snarled. 'Check all records in the region dating back as far as possible. You will need to get the guys down in archives to check the old records manually as we want checks on this individual dating back to at least 1981. You should probably also check for someone that had a lot of cash to spend. I want this done as soon as possible, so let me know when you have something.'

He hung up, a satisfied smirk appearing across his face. *This man is an enigma,* Dr Karen Laos thought to herself. She didn't know yet whether she liked him or not. He seemed to change his demeanour frequently.

Morti turned his attention back to his colleagues and checked the time on his Rolex. *Fast approaching 3.20 in the afternoon.*

'I note from Detective Constables Buzan and Carlson's visit to the students that there was nothing much to add to the witness statements given to the uniformed officers on Friday night,' he said to no one in particular.

Buzan lifted his eyes in the detective chief inspector's direction.

'That's correct, sir. The witnesses were able to add nothing further to the initial reports. Our purpose for visiting was predominantly to see the students ourselves and to introduce ourselves to them. Other than being slightly shaken up as a result of their experience on Friday night, both the two young men and the young lady appear to be sensible enough adults. As you know, Julia and her team were able to determine that the footprints found in the locality were a match to the students' trainers, importantly matching the accounts given by the group.'

He glanced at Julia Amos and she smiled a confirmatory acknowledgement.

'Other than that, we are still waiting for any news regarding tyre prints that may have been found in the area.'

Julia Amos noted her time to speak. She looked in Detective Chief Inspector Morti's direction.

'Sir, I have just recently come away from a meeting with my team in forensic science. I have some news for you all.'

Morti looked surprised, apparently not expecting to hear Julia Amos offer any input to the meeting. All of the faces in the room turned in her direction, signalling for her to continue.

'Whilst the teams down at Saline Park have not been able to definitively pull any tyre prints as such from the crime scene, they have been able to identify what we call skid marks.'

She clocked the curiosity in her colleagues' faces.

'As a result of our having been able to determine that the victim was dragged to the bushes by his killer, the teams have, early this afternoon, extended their search in an attempt to identify any vehicle prints. They started by exploring the surface of the ground in fifty metres extending from all directions of where the victim was located.' She moved her arms in a fanning motion around her as if to demonstrate. 'Ordinarily we would search further but due to the bad weather there is nothing much to go on. However, at forty-eight metres in a south-easterly direction from where the victim was found, there are definite signs of skid marks.'

Detective Inspector Roberts clarified not only for his understanding but for that of his colleagues also.

'I assume that by *skid marks* you are referring to brake patterns made from a car?'

'That is correct,' replied Amos.

'A skid mark is a tyre mark on a surface produced by a tyre that is locked, specifically one that is not rotating. A skid mark typically appears very light at the beginning of the skid getting darker as the skid progresses and comes to an abrupt end if the vehicle stops at the end of the skid. There are other types of tyre marks including scuffs, scrubs and yaw marks.

'These must not be confused with skid marks. A skid mark is left when the driver applies the brakes hard, locking the wheels, but the car continues to slide along the surface on which it is driving. Steering is not possible with the front wheels locked. Skid marks are generally straight but may have some curvature due to the slope of the approach.'

'Can you determine by these skid marks how fast the vehicle was moving in order to produce these kind of markings?' asked Detective Chief Inspector Morti, his attention focused on Julia Amos.

'That depends,' she replied, thinking quickly. 'Several things must be determined before you can establish the vehicle's skid speed. You must know the skid distance, a drag factor for the surface and the braking efficiency of the vehicle. The skid speed is the speed of the vehicle at the beginning of the visible skid mark. This will be a conservative value as the wheels do not lock up instantly. There is some "shadow skid", a light mark produced as the wheels begin to slow and just before they achieve full lock. Shadow skid and clearly visible skid should be considered as one continuous mark for any given tyre. Cars have four tyres, two in the front followed directly by the two in the rear. The wheels on most cars, assuming the brake system is functioning correctly, will tend to lock at nearly the same time. Current brake design includes pressure limiters that prevent the rear wheels from locking before the front wheels lock.

'If all four wheels lock at the same time, and the vehicle is skidding in a straight line, the marks from the rear wheels will overlap the marks from the front wheels. Rear-wheel skid marks can be identified by the dark centre while skid marks from the front wheels can be identified by two distinct thick lines on the outer edges.'

Detective Inspector James Roberts shifted in his seat and considered Julia's words.

'Can you discern the vehicle's potential age from this pattern of braking?'

'Yes, I can,' she replied. 'As I said, it is only in modern cars that pressure limiters prevent the rear car wheels from locking before the front car wheels. It is also only in cars, not motorbikes or trucks, that this type of skid-mark evidence is found. The skid marks we have identified at forty-eight metres in a south-easterly direction from where the body was found therefore tell us two things that will be important to this investigation. Firstly, that the skid marks come from a car and not any other type of vehicle and, secondly, that the car that made these markings is old. The rear wheels apparently locked before the front wheels.'

She paused as she considered her words, before adding, 'I suggest that you look for a vehicle from the 1970s to be on the safe side, although I am afraid that I am unable to tell you which model of car to look for.'.

'Isn't it possible,' asked Karen Laos, 'that the skid marks found are not from the killer's vehicle at all?'

'Yes, Dr Laos, it is entirely possible,' replied Amos. 'However, the teams down at the crime scene did not find any other markings whatsoever in the vicinity. The freshness of the skid marks and the proximity of them to the victim's body both stand as key in the conclusion that the killer did drive the victim's body to the park and that he came to a skidding halt forty-eight metres from where he dumped the victim's body. Other than that we have no additional footprints other than those of the students.'

'He bagged his feet,' added Detective Constable Carlson.

'Something like that, yes, Constable,' confirmed Julia Amos.

Detective Chief Inspector Morti had remained silent whilst Amos had delivered her findings. He was now aware of the time approaching 3.45 and the fact that the media would have started assembling in the press conference already.

'James,' he said, addressing Detective Inspector Roberts, 'I believe that you and Dr Laos are off to Wales this evening?'

Karen Laos looked across at Roberts as he replied.

'Yes, we are, sir. We have some leads to follow up with regard to the towelled gown that the victim was wrapped in. We know that the yarn used for the "Abeona" inscription could only have originated in one of three regions in Wales, namely Cardigan, Brecon and Carmarthen. I expect that we will be gone for a couple of days. We will start out by visiting farmers in the Brecon region, which is closest to Manchester.'

'Still,' interrupted Detective Constable Buzan, 'it's a good hundred and fifty miles and three hours to get there.'

'Then,' replied Detective Inspector Roberts, brushing aside the constable's words, 'let's hope that we get lucky in Brecon. If not, we will continue to Cardigan, which is approximately seventy miles from there.'

He saw Karen checking the Google map application on her phone as he spoke.

'If we get unlucky there too we will have to visit Carmarthen, fifty-four miles south of Cardigan.' He let out a deep, tired sigh. 'Either way, we have a lot of ground to cover in a short time.'

'In that case, Inspector,' interrupted Morti, 'I suggest that the two of you get moving straight after the press conference.'

He looked at Carlson and Buzan.

'And you two, please follow up on any information pertaining to William McDonald.'

'We will, sir,' replied Detective Constable Anneka Carlson.

As Karen Laos closed the Google maps application on her mobile, she saw a message flashing, indicating the arrival of a new email.

'It's a match,' she said loudly, referring to the fact that her team had successfully traced DNA from the victim's personal belongings to that of his blood.

'In that case,' retorted Detective Chief Inspector Morti, 'let's head up to see the folk from the media.'

With that, he closed the meeting. Detective Inspector Paula Stubs and Julia Amos headed back to their own offices, Trevor Stephenson disappeared into the crowded floor of the incident room, and Detective Chief Inspector Morti, Dr Laos, Detective Inspector Roberts and Detective Constables Buzan and Carlson all walked together to the lift to take them to the third floor where the press had assembled and were awaiting their arrival.

Sunday 9 October, 3.45 p.m., press conference room, Greater Manchester Police Headquarters

As the group made their way into the conference room, Detective Inspector Roberts recognized all of the members of the press that had been invited to attend the briefing. He had worked with the entire cast of them on many occasions and knew the good from the bad. He spotted seasoned and experienced journalists Camilla Johnson and John Lynn from the *Manchester Evening News* and the *Daily Mirror* respectively.

He also recognized the faces of Cyndi Smithson and Paul Butterfield from the paparazzi crowd. He had nothing against the paparazzi contingent, as long as they were really there to help his investigation rather than sensationalize it or hover around like vultures looking for a quick feed. Members of the local television station were at the back of the room, their faces less familiar to him. A small number of TV cameramen had assembled with the reporters in order to record the events that would momentarily take place. The conference was to be broadcast live on local television stations and re-run later in the evening.

A long wooden table had been assembled at the front of the room, adorned by the Manchester police logo and its phone number and the Crimestoppers number below. Five seats had been assembled neatly behind the desk, which had three jugs of water and five glasses lined up along its length. The name signs that sat in front of each seat told the group where they would be sitting. Detective Chief Inspector Morti was at the centre of the row, with the names of Detective Inspector Roberts and Dr Laos spanning the seats to his left, and those of Detective Constables Carlson and Buzan heading in a direction to the right of his chair. They each took their places as Morti started proceedings.

'Ladies and gentlemen, thank you for coming today.'

Cameras flashed and Morti's voice echoed around the hollow room as he spoke.

'We have invited you here today to ask for your help. Late on Friday night, the body of a young male was discovered in the woods and undergrowth of Saline Park, close to the border of Victoria Park, an area highly populated by students. We have over the past two days been working to identify the young victim's name and to find leads to follow in order to bring the initiator of this horrendous crime to justice.'

He certainly talks the talk. The thought crossed Dr Laos's mind unintentionally.

'As I'm sure you will understand, we are only prepared to take invited questions as this stage. I will therefore ask you for your questions in the order that I have selected names on my list.'

He indicated, with a thick thumb, the paperwork in front of him.

'I can hereby confirm the following: a group of three students making their way home late Friday night came upon the lifeless body of an eleven-year-old male. We have today been able to put a name to that victim. He was called Stephen Sanderson. Initial investigations would indicate that he was kidnapped last Monday, 3 October, whilst on a day out at the Royal Armouries close to Leeds. Stephen was a resident at a children's home in the vicinity of the Royal Armouries, his parents having died approximately one year ago in a road traffic accident.'

Karen Laos saw Detective Inspector Roberts look at her with a small tilt of his head, as if to say, *That's the first we've heard about Stephen's reasons for being in the children's home.*

'Now,' said Morti, his voice deepening as his face grew more serious, 'there are certain aspects of this case which lead us to believe that we are looking for the same person that was responsible for a very similar murder that was committed a number of years ago. That was a crime that remains unsolved.'

The silence in the room suddenly turned into an excited buzzing. Detective Chief Inspector Morti asked for quiet before he continued.

'We are obviously very busy looking at the ways in which we can track and locate the individual responsible for these crimes. We are actively pursuing leads and will continue to do so.'

He checked his list of selected members of the media that had been invited to ask questions.

'Camilla,' he said, 'from the *Manchester Evening News*, I believe that you have a question for Detective Inspector Roberts?'

Camilla Johnson stood up as a TV runner moved his boom microphone in her direction.

'Yes. Inspector Roberts, can you please give us any further details about the current victim and whether the killer you are seeking is the same person that was involved in the case known as "Peroxide Homicide" that remained unsolved several years ago?'

Her voice changed in tone as she said the words peroxide homicide.

The room grew silent, Camilla having asked the question that had been on everyone's mind since Detective Chief Inspector Morti had clarified the link between two investigations, both of which involved children.

'Thank you, Camilla,' said Detective Inspector Roberts. 'I can confirm that we are actively following that assumption.' The room hummed once more. Detective Chief Inspector Morti was careful to control the direction that the conference was taking, moving quickly to the next name on his list.

'Mr Lynn from the *Daily Mirror*. I believe that you have a question for Dr Karen Laos?'

Mr Lynn stood up, the runner with the microphone heading in his direction.

'Yes, Dr Laos, I would like to ask in what capacity you are assisting the police in their investigations and what you have discovered so far in your findings?'

'That,' replied Karen, 'is two questions, Mr Lynn. However, I will attempt to answer them appropriately.'

Detective Chief Inspector Morti shifted his weight to stare at Dr Karen Laos.

'I am assisting the police in my capacity as a consultant forensic pathologist. I was also involved in the previous case that Detective Chief Inspector Morti and Detective Inspector Roberts referred to in their respective statements. I am therefore very familiar with aspects of both cases.'

She paused and took a sip of water from the glass in front of her.

'With regard to your question about what I have discovered so far in my investigations, I can confirm that the victim found late on Friday night died at some point between midday and early evening on Friday. I am also able to confirm that the primary cause of death was strangulation, and that both ante- and post-mortem removal of parts of the victim's body took place.'

The background noise from the crowd again became more audible.

'Additionally I can confirm that the victim had been drugged prior to his death and I have detected signs of the use of hydrogen peroxide on the victim's body.'

Detective Chief Inspector Morti decided to step in.

'That, ladies and gentlemen, is the extent of our investigation so far. Please be assured that we will keep you updated over the days that follow. I am sure you understand the grave importance we place on finding the individual behind these crimes Therefore I would like to ask for your help. We would be very interested to speak to a man by the name of William McDonald.

'We know very little about this gentleman at this stage other than the fact that in 1981, 1982 and 1983 he purchased 205 litre plastic drums, each containing just less than 205,000 millilitres of hydrogen peroxide.

'These purchases were made in Oldham at a manufacturer called Jackson and Lawrence Industrial Chemical Services. The company no longer exists.'

He shifted his gaze into one of the television cameras now honed in upon him.

'We therefore appeal to all members of the public and the press to think carefully about the information we have presented during the course of this conference. We would appreciate the cooperation of all individuals in this case so that we are able to put an end to these killings and see justice served for those that have been murdered at the hands of the perpetrator so far.'

Chapter Thirteen

**Sunday 9 October, 5.10 p.m.,
M53, heading west towards Chester**

Detective Inspector James Roberts and Dr Karen Laos had been driving for a little under an hour. They had met heavy weekend traffic as they had exited Manchester on the M56. Crossing over 'the ramp', as it was affectionately called, which in reality was no more than a toll-bridge, was always a tiring and lengthy affair. Roberts had decided that it was his turn to drive, and before they had left Manchester Karen had stopped briefly at her apartment to collect a small bag of toiletries and enough clothes for two nights. *We may not be gone that long*, Roberts had told her, but she had wanted to be prepared for any eventuality.

She had felt a little apprehensive at the thought of going away with James Roberts. She found herself liking him more and more as the hours passed. They worked well together and she felt a nagging question in the back of her mind. *What will you do when all of this is over, Karen?* As she packed her bags, she had been quick to push the thought away. Roberts, waiting in his car outside, had expected to be kept waiting much longer, but Karen had returned within ten minutes.

Karen knew now as they drove towards the Welsh borders that the two of them were very much alone in their pursuit. The mortuary where she spent so much of her time felt like a distant memory. The landscape started to change as they drove through Chester and Roberts double-checked his map briefly, selecting the A483, which should have them in Brecon within two hours.

'Have you thought about where we will stay this evening?' Karen asked as the car lumbered on towards its destination.

Detective Inspector Roberts raised his eyes in a manner which indicated to her that he had not yet given any thought to their accommodation requirements. He flashed his police identification as he spoke.

'Don't worry, Karen. There will be plenty of places to choose from. I'm confident that we won't have any problems.'

Karen assumed he was right and that he had probably been in similar situation many times before. *Not exactly the same situation, not with me.* With all the excitement and rush of the past two days, Karen found that she had somewhat forgotten her initial apprehension about getting involved in the investigation and with Detective Inspector Roberts as a result.

Things seemed different now as she found herself once again alone with him. She sat back in the passenger seat and suddenly thought that Detective Inspector Roberts hadn't packed any clothes for their trip.

'James,' she said, immediately realizing that she had called the detective inspector by his first name. She quickly bit down on her tongue. He turned to meet her eyes but she had already looked away.

'Yes, Karen?' he asked.

'I didn't see you pack any clothes. Are you staying dressed like that for the next couple of days?'

She hadn't meant to sound sharp but the embarrassment she felt at having for the first time addressed him by his given name had forced the words out. Detective Inspector Roberts knew how to put her back at ease, however.

'Don't worry about me, Karen. I always have a bag packed in the boot of my car.'

His left hand tapped the dashboard as he spoke, as if he were affectionately validating his words.

'I never know where I will be heading off to at short notice,' he added. 'I keep a change of clothes, a towel and a toothbrush and toothpaste with me at all times.'

He sounded pleased with himself.

'I suppose that's a sensible precaution in your line of work,' Karen replied. 'What else do you keep in your boot?'

She didn't really know why she had asked the question but Roberts didn't appear to mind.

'I always keep a shovel in case of bad weather.' His mind recalled the items that he had packed into the back of his boot, adding 'a sleeping bag and my weapons'.

Karen recoiled at the last word he had spoken.

'Your weapons?' she asked.

'Of course,' he replied without hesitation. 'It's perfectly normal for me to carry my handcuffs, a standard-edition ASP baton, my Heckler & Koch MP5 semi-automatic and in the past few years a taser.'

Karen felt her skin bristle.

'Why do you sound more excited about the fact you have a taser in the boot than a *gun*?' she asked.

'I've been carrying a gun for years, Karen. You didn't realize that I'm an AFO?'

Authorized firearms officer. She knew the term but for some reason hadn't considered that the old-school cop who didn't even carry his handcuffs in his overcoat would ever have trained as one.

'Actually, no, I didn't,' she said. 'How long have you been carrying a gun for?'

'More than a decade now,' he said. 'It's a bit of a procedure really. I have to get re-tested every four months to make sure I'm still fit for purpose. The regional chief constable has to continually sign his authorization so that I can carry it with me.'

He paused, waiting for Karen's response, but none was forthcoming and she seemed happy enough to let him continue.

'And, before you ask, which I know you will, the answer is yes.'

'What was I going to ask you?' said Karen, feeling genuinely in the dark.

'You were going to ask whether I have ever had to use it.'

Karen struggled to picture James Roberts with a gun in his hand, let alone form an image of him in action.

'When? What happened?'

It was all she could manage to ask in response.

'The first time was just after I passed my AFO training. I was temporarily assigned to Special Branch in a counter-terrorism sting down in London.'

The first time. Karen found the image even harder to form. *That means there was a second time. Maybe more.*

'We were pursuing some suspects in an assassination plot against the Foreign Minister.'

Karen gulped down her surprise.

'And you think that what I do is interesting?'

'It's all interesting, Karen. Just different, that's all.'

'And when you used your weapon, did you kill?' she asked him.

She expected a long, drawn-out response from Roberts but found none.

'Yes, I did,' was all he said.

Karen found herself even more intrigued by her new partner; a gun-loading, armed partner.

'How do you deal with getting over that? With killing someone?' she enquired.

Roberts thought about her words carefully before replying.

'Put simply, you don't. You just deal with it as a part of the job. However bad a criminal may be, however horrible his crimes, you are still killing a living, breathing human.' He breathed deeply through his nose. 'That is something that stays with you.'

There was silence for a few seconds.

'You see, Karen, although our jobs are different, I find it difficult to imagine working with dead bodies. The very thought of draining them and examining them makes me shudder. But you do it every day, and why? Because your training allows you to do exactly that.'

Dr Laos understood his point.

'So, supposing we find our killer, would you use your gun to kill him?'

Her words brought a shiver to her spine as she spoke.

'If need be, yes, I would,' replied Detective Inspector Roberts.

After a pause, he clarified his statement.

'However, that would have to be as a last resort. We abandoned the death penalty in this country years ago and I'm not advocating its return. I'm certainly not gun-happy but if

I were in a situation where necessity called for action, then, yes, I would use my gun.'

Dr Laos checked her watch as she considered the stark reality behind Detective Inspector Roberts' words and saw the time approaching 7.30 p.m. They had been driving for nearly two and a half hours, which by her calculation put them close to Brecon. The countryside had disappeared into blackness and the encroaching night had long ago swallowed any sign of daylight. The roads were now empty. They occasionally passed a farming vehicle but other than that they were alone in the countryside of Wales.

James had noticed her checking the time and clarified their position for her benefit.

'We're only twenty-five miles out of Brecon now. We should be there shortly.'

As he finished his sentence, he saw a sign in the distance falling under the glare of his car's headlights. It read: *You are now entering Llandrindod Wells, please drive carefully.*

'Well, I don't know about you, but I'm quite happy to stop here,' said Karen, the tiredness showing around her eyes. 'I'm hungry and tired. Do you mind?'

'Of course not,' replied Roberts. 'It's as good a place as any and we can continue tomorrow morning onto Brecon.'

As they drove into the village, the street-lamps glowed a dull yellow beneath the now foggy sky. A number of pubs and restaurants dotted the main market street: all looked cosy and welcoming to the tired eyes of both Dr Laos and Detective Inspector Roberts.

'Over there,' said Karen, pointing in the direction of a pub called the White Hart Inn, which had a sign on the front door stating that bed and breakfast accommodation was available. Roberts pulled into the car park at the front and Karen saw him look longingly through the glass windows of the lounge area, where a number of large oak-framed seats and benches were clustered around a real fire.

'This looks ideal,' he said as he removed his bag from the boot of his car.

Karen had her bag in her hand already, eager to get inside. As they entered the front door, a chalk-penned menu greeted them, detailing a dozen mouth-watering options, including the dish of the day, a fish and potato grilled bake. There was no front desk so they headed into the bar area through a narrow passageway. As they emerged into the main lounge, a number of locals looked up from their tables to inspect the strangers.

Roberts led them to the bar where a large friendly-looking man, probably in his late fifties, introduced himself as Gareth, the landlord. He assumed correctly that they were looking for a room for the night.

'Welcome to Llandrindod Wells,' he said. 'Where have you driven from?'

'We're here on business, from Manchester,' Karen told him.

His small eyes peered at them through his narrow-framed glasses.

'Is that so?' he asked, his heavy Welsh accent delivering his words like a gurgling waterfall. 'You have had quite a journey in that case. How long are you looking to stay for?'

'Just the one night, please,' replied Roberts as he reached for his wallet.

'Well,' replied Gareth, 'you're in luck. We had a small influx in American tourists earlier in the day but we have one room left.'

One room left. Karen looked at Roberts in panic.

'Actually, Gareth, we were looking for two rooms,' said Detective Inspector Roberts, having interpreted Karen's facial expression.

'I'm afraid we don't have two,' said Gareth. 'Just the master bedroom on the first floor.'

Before Karen had the chance to object, Detective Inspector Roberts found himself replying, 'Well, in that case we'll take your master bedroom. To be honest, we're so tired I think we would sleep anywhere at the moment.' *Yes,* thought Karen, *but not together.* She found the prospect of sharing a bed with Roberts both frighteningly compelling whilst simultaneously objectionable. She was shocked that he'd made the decision without consulting her.

'That will be £50 for the night, please,' said Gareth, handing them a piece of paper. 'This,' he said, 'forms our standard terms and conditions for guests. I require identification from both of you, please, and payment by a credit card.'

Roberts dug into his pockets and produced his police identification. *Why didn't he just use his driving licence?* Karen thought.

Gareth seemed unfazed by Detective Inspector Roberts' force badge.

'Thank you, Detective Inspector Roberts,' he said. 'It's just the credit card now. please.'

Roberts opened his wallet and produced his credit card, asking for a receipt at the same time. *Company expenses.*

'Of course, Inspector,' said Gareth. He looked up when the transaction had gone through and asked Karen for some identification. She pulled out her driving licence and handed it over the counter.

'Thank you, *Dr* Laos,' said Gareth, his curiosity obviously piqued. 'May I ask what kind of doctor you are?'

Karen was used to the question. She had heard it countless times before. 'Of course you can ask. I'm a pathologist.'

'How interesting,' replied Gareth, before adding, 'A detective and a pathologist on the premises.'

He had spoken loudly enough for a small number of the locals sitting nearby to look up.

'I suppose you would both like something to eat and drink?' asked Gareth. His words were inviting and certainly hard to resist.

'That,' said Karen, 'sounds wonderful.'

Gareth passed Detective Inspector Roberts a key attached to a small length of wood. The room number etched into the wood told them that they would be staying in room number three.

'Up the stairs,' said Gareth, indicating to a small stairway at the end of the passage they had passed through just moments before. 'The room is on your left, about ten yards down the corridor.'

As they walked away, he called after them, 'I'll tell the chef to expect you shortly.'

They made their way back along the narrow corridor and found the staircase at the opposite end. It was equally narrow. Karen thought the building probably dated back to the eighteenth century. She had noticed, albeit briefly, that most of the buildings in the street outside looked like they were of a similar age, if not older. The staircase creaked and they had to climb single-file.

Chapter Fourteen

Sunday 9 October, 9 p.m.,
White Hart Inn, Llandrindod Wells

Detective Inspector Roberts located their room and as the door swung open, a comfortable-looking warm bedroom stretched ahead of them, an L-shape with a renovated bathroom immediately to the left of the entrance. The bed was king-size. Karen had by now decided not to say anything about Roberts' decision to opt for the single master bedroom rather than looking elsewhere in the village for somewhere to stay. She did, after all, also feel very tired.

She found herself pushing romantic thoughts out of her head. *It had been so long*. She didn't have a clue about how to even broach the subject with James Roberts. She decided to try and concentrate on getting the evening out of the way and getting back to work tomorrow morning. *Professional as always*.

'If you don't mind, James, I'll head to the shower before we go down for something to eat,' she said, picking up her bags and heading to the bathroom.

'Go for it,' said Roberts, sitting on the edge of the bed and taking his shoes off. 'I'll go after you're finished.'

Karen closed the bathroom door, relieved to have a few minutes alone. She quickly showered, the hot water pulsating through her tired and cold body as she washed away the day's build-up of stress and dust. She then cleaned her teeth and put on a comfortable evening dress, dark purple with cut-off sleeves. She applied a thin layer of makeup and took from her bag a warm cardigan, although she was hoping for a table next to the fireplace. With this in mind, she draped her cardigan over her shoulder and left the bathroom for Roberts to use.

Detective Inspector Roberts had been sitting on the end of the bed with his view fixed on the television set on the far wall. As Karen came out from the bathroom, he found himself doing a double take. *Damn, she looks beautiful,* he thought.

'Karen,' he said, 'you look amazing.'

She blushed slightly but not enough for Roberts to notice.

'Thank you, James,' she replied, sounding more confident than she felt. She was only now getting used to calling the detective inspector by his first name. *Had she overdressed?* 'Now go and have your shower so that we can finally eat something.'

As he walked to the bathroom with his bag in his hands, he resisted the urge to tell Karen that she was what he really found himself wanting to eat at that moment.

Sunday 9 October, 9.35 p.m.

Karen and James had been seated at a table close to the fireplace, much to their satisfaction. The logs on the fire crackled and spat flames from behind the grate. Karen had ordered a large glass of Australian chardonnay and James a double whisky and coke.

For dinner, Karen had selected a vegetable and chicken hotpot with a side portion of chips. She normally avoided fries or fattening foods but on this occasion she found herself relaxing and feeling hungrier than normal. The chardonnay tasted superb.

James had ordered a large steak, well cooked, with a side serving of chips and salad. He sipped on his whisky and coke and felt the pressures of the past two days dripping away. Karen felt her body warming by the fireplace and her mind somewhat tranquil for the first time in as long as she could recall.

'So, Karen,' started James, 'have you visited Wales before?'

'As a child,' she replied. 'Although I must admit that the memory is somewhat faded and distant. How about you?'

'Plenty of times,' he said, downing the last drops of his drink. He waved his arm, signalling to the waiter that he wanted a refill. 'Wales is a beautiful country but unfortunately I've only visited on business.'

The waiter arrived with a refill for James and looked at Karen's glass, which was nearly empty.

'For you, madam?' he asked.

Karen didn't usually drink much but she was surprised at how much she'd enjoyed the wine.

'Yes, please,' she replied.

Her glass was rapidly topped up by the eager waiter, the sound of the chardonnay being poured a welcome one to her ears. Their meals arrived a few moments later and both tucked in with an ardent appetite. The food was good, filling their empty and hungry bodies. A large grandfather clock in the lounge told them that the time was now 10.25 p.m.

After the meal, they decided to head back to their room. Karen stood up, the rush of the two large glasses of wine she had drunk in quick succession making her feel slightly dizzy. She found herself giggling as James leant forward to help her.

'No, I'm fine,' she said. 'But I wouldn't mind some more chardonnay. It is delicious,'

James smiled a broad grin. This was the side of Dr Karen Laos that he knew secretly existed. This was the side he had been so keen to see.

He walked over to the bar and ordered a bottle of chardonnay to take back up to their room with them. Gareth, the landlord, passed him two glasses as James paid for the meal and drinks.

As they walked out of the bar back along the narrow corridor, he called after them, 'Enjoy your evening.'

Despite her sleepiness, Karen felt somehow refreshed and invigorated. The two made their way back up the creaking staircase. Rather than climbing single file this time around, Karen found herself accepting James's outstretched hand to help her up the stairs.

When they were back in their room, James placed the two wine glasses that Gareth had given him on a dressing table close to the television, which was still on, at a low volume, the light it emitted creating a shadowy setting. Karen sat on the side of the bed and watched as James poured the wine.

He went quickly across to the bathroom and turned on the light there also, which meant that they could now both see one another fully. He returned and handed a full glass of chardonnay to Karen, which she gratefully accepted.

'Here's to partnership,' he said as they clinked glasses. He sat down on the bed next to her. 'Karen, please tell me if what I am about to say is inappropriate or unwelcome.'

Karen cocked her head to the side, waiting for him to continue and aware that her heartbeat was accelerating. She felt the blood pulsing in her neck.

'It's been a long time since I have enjoyed female company like this,' he continued. 'I know that we are colleagues but I really want to kiss you right now.'

Shocked but pleased, Karen decided in that moment to let all inhibitions go.

'Inspector,' she said. 'Are you sure you didn't plan this one bedroom being the only one available with the landlord before we arrived?' She kept an uncompromising expression as she spoke.

James clearly thought she was being serious. 'No, I would never do that!' he said, somewhat dispirited.

Karen reached down to the floor and placed her wine glass on the carpet. She turned to face him.

'James, I'm joking with you,' she said, now smiling.

Before he had the chance to reply, she had shifted her position so that she was facing him.

She reached out and took his hands to her breasts and the two began to kiss deeply and passionately. He kissed her neck and allowed his hands to explore around the top of her legs and beneath her dress.

Suddenly they were clawing one another's clothes off from their bodies and, naked, rolled on to the bed. There they made love quickly and passionately, the lust that both had kept under wraps for a long time finally finding its outlet in one another.

Neither spoke when they had finished. Karen felt renewed and full of life. She was surprised to sense that she had no regret, no guilt. She walked to the bathroom to get a towel, wrapped herself in it and then headed back around to where she had placed her wine glass. She picked it up and took a sip. James lay on top of the bed, a bedsheet now covering his genitals.

'That looks like a very good idea,' he said to Karen, watching as she continued drinking her wine.

He leant over and picked his glass up from the bedside table. They both lay quietly for ten minutes, then Karen wrapped herself under the sheets and put her arms out to find James. He reciprocated, kissed her on the forehead and said goodnight.'

Chapter Fifteen

Monday 10 October. 7.35 a.m.,
Greater Manchester Police Headquarters

Detective Constable Anneka Carlson had arrived early at
the station, leaving her house at 6 a.m. and being one of the
first to clock in for the day shift. She hadn't slept well at all.
She took her work seriously, sometimes to the detriment of
her health. She was finding Detective Inspector Roberts'
absence difficult, not purely because he was out of the area
without her but because she usually relied upon his sound
advice and liked to bounce her ideas off him. She was quite
content to be temporarily working with Detective Constable
'Fuz' Buzan but already looked forward to the time when
she would be back with the detective inspector again. She
knew that in order for that to happen this case first had to
be solved.

Although she didn't like to feel that she was being in any
way excluded, she acknowledged that Roberts was better
placed to be working with Dr Karen Laos on this case. She
wanted to do her best to help them in any way she could.
The names *Stephen Sanderson* and *William McDonald* had

tapped around her mind all night, interrupting her sleep. All she had to go on was the purchases of hydrogen peroxide that William McDonald had made in 1981, 1982 and 1983 from Jackson and Lawrence Industrial Chemical Services.

She knew that there was no way they could get any leads on the clonazepam that both victims had been drugged with prior to their deaths – that point had been made abundantly clear by Dr Joan Jackson.

So, she noted in her head, mentally checking off her to-do list, *I'm looking for someone called William McDonald, or someone that knew or knows of him. I must speak to archives this morning and see if they have had any luck with the records. I need to check with the incident room in case anyone has called in following yesterday's press conference. I'm looking for a 1970s car but that doesn't help at all. I need to find a large house with storage space. Maybe then I'll find the vehicle. I hope the inspector and Dr Laos get some leads in Wales.*

It was whilst Detective Constable Carlson was deep in thought that Detective Constable Buzan approached her desk.

'Good news, Anneka,' he said with his unmistakably excitable voice.

She looked up, now snapped out of her ponderings.

'What's good news, Fuz?'

'I've been down to the guys in archives.'

'Have they found anything?' she asked.

'Yes,' he replied. 'They found some motoring traffic charges that were brought against a William McDonald in 1984.' Anneka looked up, now genuinely interested in what Buzan was telling her.

'Mr McDonald was charged with speeding on at least

171

three different occasions in the early 1980s,' he added.

'Do we have an address for him?' asked Carlson, jumping straight to the most important question.

'Unfortunately, no, we don't,' said Buzan. 'At least not a present address. It seems that William McDonald moved to Australia at some point in 1996. A governmental census from that year was completed by Mr McDonald.'

He cleared his throat as he prepared to continue.

'This is where it starts to get interesting. The census was automatically redirected from a local post office in Rochdale and forwarded to a PO box address in Queensland, Australia. It was returned to the UK apparently signed by Mr McDonald a few months later, stating that he and his family were now permanently residing in Australia.'

'What does Rochdale have to do with any of this?' asked Detective Constable Carlson.

'I'm coming to that point. Give me time,' replied Buzan, still sounding very pleased with himself. 'Getting back to the Australia connection *first* – if William McDonald was still alive now he would be in his early nineties. The charges brought against him show his year of birth as 1920, which means that he was already in his sixties by the time he was booked for traffic offences. The guys in archives also did a bit of financial snooping.'

Anneka, whilst impressed with her partner's efforts, found herself feeling as she had when they first started working together: several paces behind.

'It seems that Mr McDonald had a cash account with the Manchester and Northern Cooperative Bank. However, the only payments that ever went into that account came not from any fixed employment but from a counterpart bank in Brisbane, Australia. Every month a sum totalling the equivalent of £1,500 was transferred to the account here in the UK.'

He paused as he scanned his notepad.

'The interesting thing is that from 1996 regular withdrawals from the UK end ceased. The money is still transferred monthly into the Manchester and Northern Cooperative and has been only sparingly withdrawn over the subsequent years.'

'If William McDonald moved to Australia in 1996, then who has been withdrawing the cash from this end?' asked Detective Constable Carlson.

'We need to speak to the bank,' replied Buzan.

Anneka thought about what Buzan had said and something didn't seem right in her mind. After a moment of contemplating his words, she spoke up again.

'How could a seventy-six-year-old man move to Australia?' she asked. 'Surely he wouldn't have passed any of the strict Australian medicals or immigration procedures.'

'That's exactly what I thought,' replied Buzan. 'I ran a check on his family and it turns out that his wife was an Australian citizen.'

I'm not the only one that started early today, Anneka thought.

'Her family name was Maria Lopez,' he added. 'The records indicate that the two of them had one son, called Kurt McDonald. He moved with his family aged sixteen to Australia. However, when I contacted our colleagues in immigration, they couldn't find any official documents pertaining to a family by the name of McDonald having moved to Australia at that time.'

'So how is it possible for the McDonalds' bank account to have been receiving such frequent transfers from Australia?'

asked Carlson. 'And who has been sending so much money?'

'That,' said Buzan, 'is something we will have to figure out.'

Anneka tapped her pen on her desk as she swivelled around in her chair.

'You said just now that we don't have a *present* address for William McDonald. What does Rochdale have to do with all of this?'

Detective Constable Buzan opened his notepad and checked his information.

'Well, the family apparently owned a house out in Rochdale before they somehow moved or disappeared.' He squinted as he thought. 'But that house no longer exists. When William McDonald was charged with speeding in the 1980s he stated that he and his wife paid for their house in cash in the late 1960s.'

'That fits with what the detective chief inspector said about someone being cash rich and having been in a position to buy hydrogen peroxide in the quantities that Dr Jackson indicated,' said Carlson. 'What do you mean that the house no longer exists?'

'Well, there are no known records of the house that McDonald listed as his residence when he was booked for speeding offences. He stated that he lived at Manor House in Dutchy Street, Rochdale. I have checked and there are no streets that exist by that name, nor are there any signs that a Manor House ever existed.'

'So,' concluded Carlson, 'he lied about his address when he appeared in court for the motoring offences.'

'That would certainly make sense,' agreed Buzan.

'I suppose if someone had enough cash they could have quite easily moved overseas if they had a reason to pay someone to hide their migration,' Carlson said.

Buzan concurred with his partner's reasoning.

'But why would they need to hide their migration? His wife was an Australian citizen, which means that by default he would have had the right to move with her and their son would most certainly have had the right to move with his parents to his mother's homeland. Besides, it's not as if they had serious criminal records. It was a simple motoring charge.'

Detective Constable Carlson turned her thoughts back to the previous day's press conference.

'Did any members of the public respond overnight to the press conference from yesterday?' she asked.

'Not that I have heard of,' said Duban. 'But we can check this morning with the incident room to be sure. You know how things sometimes don't get reported to us until we check in person.'

A frustrating truth, Carlson thought.

'OK,' she said. 'But before we do that let's pull up some maps of this Manor House area and see if we're missing anything. Something doesn't feel right about this. And get me the info on the transfer between bank accounts. We need to speak to the Australian end and find out who has been making these transfers. I want to know who transferred money between those accounts and who owns them now.'

She seems a little irritable today, Buzan thought, but moved off to get the records that she had asked for. As he left the room, Anneka shouted after him.

'I'm going to email the detective inspector and let him know about the Rochdale connection.'

*

Monday 10 October, 8.10 a.m.,
White Hart Inn, Llandrindod Wells

Dr Karen Laos had woken earlier than Detective Inspector Roberts and it had been the sound of her taking a morning shower than had stirred him from his sleep. He had expected that Karen would act uncomfortably following their intimacy but was now surprised and rather pleased to find that she maintained their new closeness.

'Morning, James!' she called from the bathroom upon hearing him get out of bed. 'How did you sleep?'

'Like a baby,' he said. 'You?'

As she dried her hair and dressed back into her smart work clothes, she looked at herself in the mirror, quite impressed that she didn't feel worse for wear after her chardonnay intake.

'It was just what I needed,' she replied.

She quickly realized that what she had said could be interpreted in different ways. James heard her chuckling to herself in the bathroom.

'I meant the sleep was just what I needed,' she clarified.

'And how about the other?' asked James, playing along.

'That,' said Karen, not wanting to embarrass her colleague, 'was also very welcome.'

Diplomatic and polite, he thought.

She emerged from the bathroom looking refreshed and ready for a long day's work.

'The bathroom is all yours,' she said as she began to pack her bags.

'Thank you,' the inspector replied. As he closed the door behind him, he added, 'Let's go down for coffee before we head off to Brecon.'

That sounds like an excellent idea, Karen thought as she heard James starting the shower.

In the light of the morning, the bar downstairs had a very different feel about it. The romanticism of the previous night had by default dissipated as their thoughts returned to the work they had ahead of them. They both skipped the full breakfast option, deciding instead to have coffees. James pulled a map from his bag and put it on the table in front of them.

He indicated to Karen the distance they had to go to reach their first destination.

'We are here,' he said, his right forefinger tapping an area on the map. 'We need to head south for another twenty-five miles to reach Brecon.'

'And what are we going to do when we get there?' asked Karen.

'Simply put, speak to some farmers about Balween sheep,' replied James.

The landlord, Gareth, was hovering in the background and had overheard their conversation. He approached their table on the pretence of refilling their half-empty coffee cups.

'No, thank you, I'm done for now,' said Karen.

James agreed, feeling the kick he had needed from the caffeine.

'Inspector,' said Gareth, 'I wasn't eavesdropping on your conversation but I think I heard you say the word Balween just now?'

'That's right, Gareth,' replied Roberts. 'Why do you ask?'

Gareth pulled a chair up to their table and sat down, speaking in a low voice.

'It's been many years that I haven't heard that name,' he

started. 'I grew up in Brecon, you see, and my late uncle on my father's side was a farmer. He used to talk endlessly about Balween when I was a small boy.'

Detective Inspector Roberts didn't dare to imagine that they could have got so lucky so early into their search, although both he and Dr Laos secretly hoped that they wouldn't have to drive across the country to Cardigan and Carmarthen.

'Is that so?' asked Detective Inspector Roberts. 'What did he say about this type of sheep?'

Gareth looked as if he had just been asked the most important question in the world.

'What *didn't* he say? That would be a more suitable question, Inspector.' He half whispered his words across the table. 'He used to tell me about how hard he had worked to help save this native sheep. Apparently there was a time back in the 1940s when the local farmers were more concerned with saving the Balween than they were with winning the war.'

'Really?' asked Detective Inspector Roberts. 'It just so happens that we are looking for some farmers that have very specialized knowledge of the Balween.'

Gareth pulled himself in closer still to the table, his body now firmly between Dr Laos and Detective Inspector Roberts. 'In that case you need to speak to my cousin Aled,' he said. 'He took over the farm after my uncle passed on, God rest his soul. And he learnt everything he knows about the Balween from our grandmother. She's still alive but not very coherent, I'm afraid. But if she's having a good day she could talk to you for hours about the Balween.'

That's exactly what we need, thought Karen.

Gareth took a pen and paper from his overalls and started

to write the name and address of his cousin Aled. 'Of course, farming isn't what it used to be,' he added. 'That's why I chose the pub trade.' A sparkle appeared in his eyes as he spoke. 'Can I ask why you want to know about the Balween?'

Karen looked at Detective Inspector Roberts and he returned her glance. She saw her chance to step in. 'It's just part of an investigation we are following up,' she said. 'You see, there was a terrible crime committed and we are trying to trace the individual responsible for that crime. Your input would go a very long way in helping this investigation.'

She spoke seriously and endeared herself to Gareth.

Way to go, girl, Roberts thought.

'Really?' asked Gareth excitedly 'In that case I'll go and give Aled a call now and tell him to expect you.'

He wrote the name 'Bevan's Farm' and some local directions on the piece of paper before moving off from the table.

'Not a bad start,' the inspector said to Dr Laos.

'Indeed,' she replied. 'Let's see what this Aled and the grandmother have to say, if she can tell us anything at all. I think that we have a one in three chance of finding the source of the yarn from the Balween. They don't seem like bad odds to me.'

'I agree,' said James. 'Let's just hope that the grandmother remembers either a visitor from the north of England that used to go and buy Balween wool or someone that ordered the same back in 1935.'

Gareth returned after a few moments had passed, a wide smile on across his face.

'I have told Aled to expect a visit from an inspector and a pathologist,' he said. 'Needless to say he was a little surprised when I told him you wanted to know about the Balween. He has a healthy herd of them now.'

Detective Inspector Roberts stood up and thanked their host. As they left the pub, their bags in their hands, Gareth stood at the door waving them farewell, his smile fixed in place.

Monday 10 October, 8.10 a.m.,
Greater Manchester Police Headquarters

'This is a map of Rochdale from 1988,' said Detective Constable Buzan, making space on the large desk in front of him. He laid open the yellow-stained map so that Anneka Carlson could see it as well.

'Rochdale is situated exactly five point three miles north by north-west of Oldham, from where we know that William McDonald purchased his hydrogen peroxide.'

'So,' replied Anneka, 'the distance would check out as a starting point.'

'Exactly,' agreed Buzan. 'Rochdale is also situated within the target area we are considering, laying in a north by north-easterly direction from Manchester itself.'

Detective Constable Anneka Carlson nodded her head in agreement.

'Here is the main town,' said Buzan.

Anneka nodded once more as he moved his finger over grid reference B-6.

'That looks pretty much the same as it does these days,' she said. 'However, as I recall there are several newer housing estates that should be located about here.'

She indicated in grid B-7 where she knew houses and developments had been constructed since the 1990s.

Buzan agreed with her assessment.

'Either I am missing a large section of this map, or Dutchy Street never existed and was simply made up by Mr McDonald at the time of the charges being brought against him for motoring offences,' he said.

Anneka looked carefully at all grid sections of the map, most of which were simply filled by different coloured boxes and squares indicating fields and forestry.

'Is there any way we can get an earlier map?' she asked.

'Just in case things changed between the time McDonald claimed to have bought the property in the 1960s and the time this map was produced in 1988?'

Buzan reached down beneath the desk and pulled an official ordnance survey map from 1954 out of a cardboard box that had sat in archives for decades. The colour was even more faded yellow than the previous map from 1988.

'This is a map from thirty-four years before the last,' he said.

He moved the 1988 map out of the way temporarily whilst he opened the map from 1954.

'As you can see, it's pretty damaged but the basic structure of Rochdale hasn't changed in any unexpected ways. Of course, many of the buildings such as the bakeries and butchers indicated here no longer exist due to modernization.'

As he spoke, he moved his finger along the old grid-reference number A-1, which covered the town centre.

Detective Constable Anneka Carlson followed his finger and saw it stop, indicating that he felt there was little more they would be able to achieve by staring down at dusty old maps. She looked at a small section of the map that included alphabetical street names.

'No mention of a Dutchy Street here either,' she said, feeling somewhat deflated. 'Let's have a look at the bank accounts; maybe we will find something there of interest.'

Detective Constable Buzan pulled out what little paper-work he had managed to obtain from their colleagues in archives.

'This is a bank statement that Mr McDonald gave to the officers who booked him for traffic offences back in the 1980s. Although he only gave this copy to the officers at the time, archives have been able to obtain proof that the account is still active to the current day and still receives the same amount of money each month. As I said before, the withdrawals have been irregular and sparse since 1996. As you can see, there is no address on the bank statement. It simply states "Mr William McDonald, care of the Manchester and Northern Cooperative Bank". It seems that William McDonald had his statements held by the bank and only collected them when he needed them, an option commonly available now but one that at the time was quite rare.'

Detective Constable Carlson looked at the bank statement and noticed that it covered six months, covering the first half of 1982. Each month showed a transfer of the equivalent of £1,500, initiated by a bank under the name of Brisbane and Bribie Building Society. Detective Constable Carlson picked up her mobile phone and clicked on the internet icon. She navigated to her Google homepage and entered the bank's name. The page loaded for several seconds before the search was complete.

'Here we go,' she said to Detective Constable Buzan, who was watching over her shoulder. 'Brisbane and Bribie Building Society.'

She clicked on the address bar and waited whilst the page loaded. She then clicked on the 'contact us' option and made a note of the phone number. She made a quick calculation in her head and worked out that the current time in Brisbane, Australia was approaching 6.45 p.m. They were ten hours behind Australia at this time of the year. She reached for the landline from the desk, clearing the old maps out of her way, and dialled the number.

'You realize, Anneka, that we may need the assistance of the police out there to find out who owns this account?' said Buzan.

Anneka ignored his words and continued dialling. It rang briefly before connecting to an automatic menu. She pushed the number two as instructed in order to speak to a customer service representative.

She checked the account numbers, underlining both the sender's account in Australia and the recipient's account in the UK. A shrill female voice answered the call.

'Good evening, you're speaking to Melina. How can I help you?'

Carlson winked at Buzan as she started to speak.

'Yes, good evening, Melina. This is Detective Constable Anneka Carlson. I am calling you from Greater Manchester Police Headquarters in the UK. My colleagues and I are currently investigating a murder and we need to ask you to run a trace on an account that is registered with your bank.' She didn't want to give Melina a chance to get spooked and make some excuse, so she continued. 'If you would like me to give you the account number, I have it here with me.'

Melina was silent for a few seconds whilst she registered Anneka's words.

'That will be fine, Constable,' she said. 'Normally we would not be able to assist with queries like this unless they come via the local police. However, you said that you have the account number with you?'

'Yes,' replied Carlson, now feeling more confident. 'We have the account number and transaction codes that show that a certain amount of money has been transferred from an account held with your bank to the Manchester and Northern Cooperative Bank here in the UK on a monthly basis since at least 1982.'

'Please give me the account number you have for the Australian account,' said Melina, whose voice, despite coming from more than ten thousand miles away, was sharp and clear.

'The local account number is 23548974.'

'Please hold,' said Melina, waiting for her system to load.

Buzan looked expectantly at Anneka as they awaited the outcome.

'That account, Constable,' said Melina, 'is registered to a Geraldine Lopez.'

Lopez. The name matched that of William McDonald's wife.

'Thank you, Melina,' said Carlson. 'I wonder. Can you clarify that the payments from your end have been directed to a gentleman by the name of William McDonald?'

'My system shows that the money that has been transferred indicates the payee's name as Maria Lopez.'

She paused and corrected herself.

'Sorry, there are two payees. The primary payee was initially Maria Lopez in 1966 but ten years later we were instructed by Maria Lopez to add her then husband, William McDonald, as a secondary payee. He was therefore authorized to access the account from your end.'

Detective Constable Buzan scribbled a small note with the words *'How were the two Lopezes related?'* He passed it to Anneka. She nodded her head to show her colleague that she understood what he wanted her to ask.

'Thank you, Melina. You have been a great deal of help to us,' said Carlson. 'I have just one last question for you.'

She took a breath and continued.

'Do you have any information on your system that tells you the nature of the relationship between Maria and Geraldine Lopez, or even better an address for Geraldine Lopez?'

'I'm sorry, Constable, but I can't tell you that. The records are very old and I only have access to those that are electronically stored. I would suggest that you speak to the police here in Brisbane.'

Detective Constable Carlson knew that she had exhausted her line of enquiry with Melina and took the hint. She didn't feel that she was being brushed off; just that Melina really couldn't access any other information on her system. She thanked Melina again for all her help and ended the call.

'What do you suggest we do now?' asked Buzan.

'Now, Fuz,' replied Anneka, 'we contact the police in Brisbane and ask for their help.'

In Detective Inspector Roberts' absence, she picked up her phone and dialled Detective Chief Inspector Morti's extension to update him on their progress. She checked her watch and saw that it was still very early. She waited as the phone rang, half expecting that he might not be at his desk yet. She was about to put the phone down when Morti answered. Detective Constable Buzan listened as Anneka ran through what they had discovered with regard to William McDonald, his family, where he might have lived and her conversation with the bank in Brisbane, Australia.

She gave Buzan a thumbs-up, which told him that they had the go-ahead to call the Australian police. He opened a drawer on the desk and pulled out a police-issued phone directory with all the names and international numbers they would need in such investigations. He then picked up a high-lighter pen off the table and scanned through the country guide, finding Australia. He underlined the number he was looking for, which appeared next to *'Brisbane Criminal Investigation Department'*.

Chapter Sixteen

Monday 10 October, 9 a.m.,
A470 to Brecon

As Detective Inspector James Roberts drove along the small country roads that wound their way through the Welsh countryside, Dr Karen Laos held in her hand the pencil-scribbled directions that Gareth had provided them with so that they could find his sheep-farming cousin, Aled, and his elderly grandmother. The early-morning fog had started to lift as a crack of hazy sunshine broke through the sky. *The worst time of the year,* Karen thought, grateful for the car's central heating and her warm scarf. The fields that expanded in all directions were dull and grey and the greenery that would have been aplenty in the summer months now long dead with the waning of the seasons.

James noticed a sign indicating the B4602 that would take them straight into Brecon.

'We need to turn off just after this sign,' said Karen, studying Gareth's sketch.

'And there it is,' said James, as he turned the car a sharp left into a narrow dirt track with the sign *'Bevan's Farm'* hanging below a rusted metallic gateway.

He decreased his speed as the car made its way along a 100-metre stretch of waterlogged pathway.

'I guess they must have a larger exit road for the farm vehicles,' said Karen as she looked around.

'This *is* the private entrance,' Inspector Roberts replied. He smiled as he spoke.

At the end of the track they saw a large farmhouse looming out from behind several thorny bushes and trees. A spiral of smoke from the chimney on the roof indicated the presence of a coal-burning fire within.

Detective Inspector Roberts pulled his car into a small space at the front of the house. As they exited the vehicle, they spotted a man coming out from the front door. He looked remarkably like Gareth and they assumed that this was Aled. He wore green waders that extended from his feet all the way up to his waist. *Much needed in these conditions,* James thought as he walked towards the man. His jumper was a thick fleece which Karen automatically assumed had come from his own Balween herd. The farm was quiet and in the distance she could hear the sounds of animals grazing. She looked around but couldn't see the elusive Balween.

'I assume that you are the inspector and the doctor my cousin Gareth told me about,' the man said as he approached them both.

Karen introduced herself first, remarking on how beautiful she found his farm. He had the same friendly plump face as Gareth but his accent was far deeper than his cousin's.

'Gareth tells me you want to know about the Balween. He also told me that he thinks the fact you're both here from Manchester must mean that you're working on something you consider urgent.'

He was clearly equally as curious as his landlord cousin had been by the two strangers' visit.

'In a manner of speaking that is correct, sir. Your cousin was polite enough not to ask us exactly why we are here asking all these questions but the fact is that we are working on solving a murder case. We're in Wales in order to look for evidence that wool from the Balween sheep was used in a recent murder that happened in Manchester,' clarified Detective Inspector Roberts.

Aled now looked intensely inquisitive. 'You mean to say that the wool from one of my Balween is connected to a dead body?' he asked.

Friendly but not all that bright, Karen found herself thinking. She stepped forward.

'No, sir, what my colleague means is that a murder victim was found dressed in clothing that had yarn in it, which we have determined came from the wool of a Balween. We're not saying that the wool definitely came from one of your sheep but we do know that there are only three regions in Wales where the Balween is found.'

'That's correct,' said Aled. 'Here in Brecon and further west in Cardigan and Carmarthen.'

'How long has your family been working with the Balween sheep?' asked Detective Inspector Roberts.

Aled did not hesitate in answering. 'For as long as anyone of us can recall,' he said. 'My father and his parents were farming the Balween long before any of us were alive.'

He moved his hands around as he spoke, as if he were inviting his guests to look at his farm.

'And do you know for how long the other farmers in Cardigan and Carmarthen have been raising the Balween?' continued Roberts.

'Why does that matter?' asked Aled.

'Because,' said Roberts, 'we are trying to find a farm that has been producing the Balween for at least seventy years.'

Aled's face lit up in delight, clearly keen to show off his heritage.

'You should have said so, Inspector. *We* are the only family of farmers that have been working with the Balween for that long that I know of. A lovely sheep it is.'

'I'm sure that is so, sir,' said Karen, trying to accelerate their meeting. 'I'm sure you can appreciate the urgency of our visit. Now that you have been able to clarify that your family is the only family you are aware of that has worked with the Balween for so long, we can tell you more specifically about why we are here.'

Detective Inspector Roberts looked at her, inherently trusting her professionalism and allowing her to participate. He watched as Karen continued to explain the purpose of their visit.

'Aled, this is a bit of a long shot but we are trying to find out whether you have any records whatsoever relating to sales from your Balween wool from seventy years ago.'

Aled thought for several seconds before answering.

'Well, I obviously wasn't alive seventy years ago and I am afraid that we didn't keep receipts back then. However, if anyone can help you it would be my grandmother, Nerys Bevan.'

Roberts recalled the name on the rusting sign to the farm's entrance. *Bevan's Farm.*

'Your cousin Gareth tells us that your grandmother isn't very well,' said Karen. 'I am very sorry to hear that, but do you think she might be willing to speak to us?'

'You can try,' replied Aled. 'Although she isn't always very coherent; the doctors call it dementia.'

He said the words as if they were new to him.

Aled walked towards the front door of the farmhouse and gestured for his guests to follow. He swung open a large heavy oak door that led immediately into the living room. There, sat in a chair possibly as old as she, facing the fireplace, was his grandmother, Nerys Bevan. Her eyes were closed. Aled went over to speak to her.

'Nanny,' he said, gently tapping her on the shoulder. 'There are some guests here that would like to speak to you.'

She half opened her eyes.

'Peter, is that you?' she replied, with a voice both croaky and deep.

Aled turned to his guests. 'She often thinks that I am her late husband.'

Karen approached Nerys Bevan herself and bent down to speak to her.

'Mrs Bevan, my name is Karen and this is my friend James.'

She pointed with her right hand to indicate the inspector's presence as he too came closer.

'Why are you in my house?' asked Nerys, waking from her daydreams. 'What do you want from me?'

Karen recognized the irritability and hesitation in her voice as classic signs of dementia. She recalled her own place-ment in psychiatry as a medical student. Karen looked at Aled and quietly spoke to him.

'Perhaps it would help, Aled, if you showed your grand-mother something that is very familiar to her.'

Aled turned and opened a drawer. He pulled out a ball of yarn.

'She used to love knitting,' he said. 'On good days she still can.'

He spoke with both pride and sadness. Karen took the yarn from Aled's hands and placed it in his grandmother's lap.

She watched as Nerys's gnarled fingers reached for the yarn. She waited until she was sure that Nerys recognized it and again approached her.

'Do you knit often, Mrs Bevan?' she asked.

Nerys looked up at her, this time seemingly more oriented than she had been before.

'Aled,' she said, now recognizing her grandson. 'Why didn't you tell me that we have guests? Offer the young lady something to drink.'

James hid a contented grin as he watched the way in which Karen's soothing actions had helped Mrs Bevan. Aled moved to offer Karen something to drink but she signalled to him that she was fine.

'Mrs Bevan, I hope you don't mind, but your grandson Aled tells me that you are somewhat of an expert on the Balween sheep and I really want to know more about them,' she said to the old lady.

Mrs Bevan's face came to life at hearing the word Balween. Her eyes opened fully for the first time and she lifted the ball of yarn in her hands.

'This, young lady, is from a Balween.'

Karen recognized the fibre from the ones that she had seen on the victims.

'The Balween is a beautiful sheep, young lady. There is nothing else quite like it. My, it has the most wonderful colours of white on its face and tail, hidden beneath the brown and black of its main coat.'

Her eyes and face were now both animated as she spoke.

'The Welsh really love their Balween,' she continued.

Karen wanted to let her speak but knew that there wasn't enough time for a history lesson. Keeping to the same subject, she changed tactic slightly.

'How about the English?' she asked. 'Do they know anything about the Balween?'

Nerys Bevan looked surprised at the question. 'Not many.' She chuckled. 'Though I did once have a good friend from England that tried to learn about the Balween. She used to come and visit my farm just to buy its wool.'

Roberts looked at Karen and she registered his urgency.

'What was your friend's name, Mrs Bevan?' Karen asked.

The old lady thought long and hard. 'She had a funny name, like the storybook *e-i-e-i-o.*'

'The farmer?' asked Karen. 'As in old McDonald had a farm, *e-i-e-i-o?*'

She half sung the last few words, to help Mrs Bevan's recollection.

Mrs Bevan's deep laugh told Karen that she was right. 'Yes! That's it,' she said. 'Old McDonald.'

Roberts took out his notepad and wrote 'affirmative link' next to the name of William McDonald.

'What was her first name, Mrs Bevan?' Karen asked.

The old lady drew a blank again.

'Whose first name, my dear?'

'The English lady you said used to come and ask you about the Balween sheep. You said that she used to come to see you from England.'

Nerys Bevan caught onto the conversation once more but seemed slightly more confused again.

'Yes, as I told you, she used to visit me from Manchester. She would come here and buy the Balween wool. Huge quantities of it,' she added. 'I helped her learn how to knit, you know.'

Aled's face looked blank. This was clearly the first time he had ever heard this story. Karen pushed on.

'And her first name; the lady from Manchester whose surname was McDonald?'

Nerys Bevan looked down at the Balween yarn in her hands and suddenly said, 'Edna. Edna McDonald. She was a good friend of mine, you know. She used to write to me often, even after she stopped coming here to buy the wool. She had a terrible son, though. He moved her into his house when she got old.'

Detective Inspector Roberts felt sure they were getting very close to finding their suspect. The links were making sense and the loose ends beginning to tie together. He pulled out his mobile phone and scanned the most recent email update he had from Detective Constable Carlson. She had, as always, been sure to include all concerned parties into the email. He read her email.

William McDonald was booked for speeding in the early 1980s. He may have given a fake address in Rochdale. He claimed he lived at Manor House in Dutchy Street but there is no evidence of any such address. He and his wife, Maria Lopez, had a shared bank account with the Manchester and Northern Cooperative into which money was transferred every month from Australia. He appears to have moved to Australia in 1996 with his Australian wife and their son, Kurt. No evidence to confirm either way. We have spoken to the Australian bank and later we will talk with the local police. The name Geraldine Lopez needs checking.

'Mrs Bevan,' said Karen. Do you have the letters that Edna McDonald sent you?'

She was hoping they would be able to pull an address from the correspondence. Detective Inspector Roberts was listening eagerly. The old lady looked deep in thought once more.

'Somewhere, my dear,' she replied.

Aled stepped forward. 'Nanny,' he said. 'Maybe those letters are in your case up in the attic?'

Nerys Bevan looked at her grandson but drew a blank.

Inspector Roberts ushered Aled to the side.

'I am sure you understand how important it is that we see those letters just in case there is an address we can use,' he said quietly, before adding, 'and of course how very grateful we would be to you, sir.'

Aled, somewhat taller than Roberts, stooped down to reply. 'Of course, Detective,' he said. 'I will head up to the attic a bit later but it is a real mess up there and I don't even know if I will be able to find her stuff.'

He paused.

'I haven't been up there in years.'

Detective Inspector Roberts slipped Aled his business card.

'On here you will find my mobile and office number. There is also a fax number. If you could please contact me as soon as you have any information either way. My colleague and I need to head back up to Manchester very shortly.'

Aled nodded to show the inspector that he understood the urgency of the request.

'If I find the letters, I will ask the local police in the village to fax them to you immediately,' he said.

'For that,' replied Roberts, 'I would be very, very grateful.'

Karen stood up from her kneeling position, patted the old lady's hand and whispered 'thank you'.

With that, she and Roberts headed through the front door and back to their car. Roberts started the engine and neither spoke as they made their way back along the narrow dirt-track that would lead them to the exit from the farm. Stopping just shy of the main road, Roberts pulled the car to a gentle stop.

He turned to Karen.

'I'm satisfied that we can head back to Manchester now. Detective Constable Carlson and Detective Constable Buzan have confirmed the McDonald family link in Rochdale although they haven't been able to get an address.'

He bit down on his lower lip as he thought.

'Somebody has gone to great lengths to disguise the so-called house that the family supposedly lived in. If we can just get an address from Aled for where this Edna McDonald claimed she lived with her son William in her latter years, we can pounce.'

Karen contemplated the word *pounce*, feeling too that they were getting closer to finding their killer.

'And what do you expect to find there,' she asked, 'if the family really did move away to Australia in 1996?'

Roberts spoke gravely.

'*Anything* that will help us find what we're looking for.'

He started the car's engine, more sharply than usual, and checked the time.

It was 10 a.m.

'We should make it back to Manchester by 12.30,' he said to Karen.

'You're being optimistic, aren't you?' she replied.

'Oh, there's life in the old dear yet,' he said as he fondly tapped the dashboard of his vehicle.

Karen smiled and sat back in her seat as Detective

Inspector Roberts pulled away through the narrow country lanes.

Monday 10 October, 1.15 a.m., Greater Manchester Police Headquarters

Detective Constable 'Fuz' Buzan had taken responsibility for calling the cops in Brisbane while Anneka Carlson went to get herself a coffee. He dialled the number that he had previously highlighted and had the name of Geraldine Lopez and her bank account number next to him. The line rang for a minute and a half before a heavy Queensland accent answered at the other side. The man introduced himself as Inspector Stamatis. Buzan didn't know for sure but he guessed that the name had descended from Greek origins. Inspector Stamatis sounded as if he were in his late forties, maybe early fifties.

'Inspector,' said Buzan, after explaining the purpose of his call, 'any help you can provide us with would be greatly appreciated. We really need to clarify that a Geraldine Lopez has been making payments into a UK bank account.'

He gave the inspector both the account number in the UK, held by the Manchester and Northern Cooperative Bank, and that of the account held in Australia by the Brisbane and Bribie Building Society. The inspector input the information and confirmed to Buzan that he had a name and address of a Geraldine Lopez.

'She lives quite a way out, Constable,' he said. 'It's getting pretty late here so I'm afraid we will only be able to send an officer down to see her in the morning, which will be your evening.'

Buzan checked the time and worked out that with the ten-hour differential he might expect to hear back early to mid evening that day.

'I appreciate your help, Inspector. Please can you ask your officers to ascertain from Mrs Lopez how she knows Maria Lopez and William McDonald?'

The inspector confirmed that he would ensure the message was passed along.

'We also need to know why Geraldine has been continuing to send payments through to the UK bank account when we are not even sure where the McDonalds live now, here or in Australia.' He paused before adding, 'Or indeed whether they are still alive.

'We do know that on rare occasions the money has been withdrawn from the UK side but very infrequently since 1996. What we don't know is by whom.'

The inspector promised he would do all he could to help and would get back in touch within the next twelve hours.

Chapter Seventeen

Monday 10 October, 11.30 a.m.,
Greater Manchester Police Headquarters

Detective Constable Anneka Carlson was deep in thought as she walked through the police incident room and at first didn't notice the young police constable waving at her from a desk where he had been manning the telephones all morning. She headed in his direction and saw him place the phone he was holding on mute.

'There is a lady on the phone asking to speak to Detective Inspector Roberts regarding yesterday's press conference.'

Carlson stepped forward. 'I'll take it, Constable, thank you.'

He handed her the phone.

'Hello,' she said, 'This is Detective Constable Anneka Carlson. I believe you want to speak with someone regarding the press conference from yesterday?'

A quiet, female voice replied.

'Yes, I think I may have some information that can help you in your investigation.'

Anneka took a pen and notepad from the desk she was

now standing behind.

'Can I have your name, please?' she asked.

'Yes. My name is Rebecca Mayfield.'

Carlson made a note.

'How can we help you, Rebecca?'

'Well . . .' she said hesitantly. 'You said yesterday that you wanted to speak to somebody called William McDonald?'

'That's correct,' replied Detective Constable Carlson. 'Do you know the gentleman?'

'Not personally but I think my mother did,' said Rebecca.

'What do you mean, you think your mother may have known him?' enquired Carlson.

'Well,' said Rebecca, after a pause, 'my mother passed away several years ago but she told me about a family that lived close to us and I definitely recall that the father's name was William McDonald.'

Carlson made a few notes before replying.

'And where is it that you live, Rebecca?' she asked.

'I live in Rochdale.'

Rochdale, the very area they had drawn a blank in so far. Detective Constable Carlson let her continue.

'My mother's name was Cecily Mayfield. She knew a William and Maria McDonald many years ago.'

Maria. The name hit her fast as she pieced together Maria McDonald, previously Lopez.

'Apparently Maria was rarely seen and was very sick. My mother told me that they were a strange family and kept themselves to themselves. I was very young when they moved to Australia.'

'Can you confirm that the family moved to Australia, Rebecca?' she asked. 'We have heard contradictory reports regarding that.'

'Well, I can only confirm that the family seemed to disappear in the mid 1990s and we received a thank you letter from Maria McDonald a few months later that said she and her husband had decided to move with their son to Australia as her health was continuing to deteriorate.'

'What was her health problem?' asked Anneka.

'Apparently she had multiple sclerosis. Mum told me that she had been sick for a long time and that she had helped her as much as possible by giving her medication.' She paused. 'Her husband, strangely, never seemed very happy that my mother had tried to help. The letter from Maria said that she wanted to spend her retirement closer to her family in Australia, especially her youngest sister, Geraldine, who she hadn't seen in years.'

Bingo, thought Carlson. *So, Geraldine is or was Maria's sister. The very same Geraldine that owns the Brisbane and Bribie Building Society account.*

'What kind of medication did your mother give to Maria McDonald?' she asked Rebecca.

'My mother was an epileptic and her doctor had prescribed a drug that she said made her too drowsy so she never took it but was too afraid to tell her doctor. She kept cashing in her prescriptions to keep the doctor happy and finally gave it all away to Mrs McDonald but I'm afraid I don't remember the drug's name.'

Anneka felt her heart start to beat faster.

'If I asked you if that drug was called clonazepam, would that ring a bell?' she pressed.

'Yes, that's the one!' answered Rebecca. 'How did you know that?'

'I'm afraid that at this stage I can't say. However, please do tell me more about the McDonald family, Rebecca, especially where they lived.'

'As I said, Constable, I don't know too much about the family but I certainly know where they lived.'

'Rebecca,' said Carlson, 'the name of the street that the family lived in is very important for us to know. We have been told that they may have lived in a street by the name of Dutchy Street. Have you heard of that?'

'Dutchy Street?' asked Rebecca. 'No, I have never heard of that street.'

So, the name of the street was all a ruse, Anneka thought. Rebecca continued.

'The family lived in a very large house and it was extremely difficult to even see the place unless you were actually invited there in person. It had about ten acres of land with it.'

The house description matches that given by the forensic psychologist, thought Carlson.

'Rebecca, you said that the house *was* very difficult to see and that it *had* lots of land. Do you mean that it no longer exists?'

'No,' replied Rebecca immediately. 'The house is certainly still there. I assume that the McDonald family kept it after they moved to Australia as I have sometimes seen activity there.'

Carlson felt that she was making progress.

'What kind of activity have you seen?' she asked.

'Well, not much. Just the occasional sign of a dull light coming from across the fields. I don't see it often, and I always assumed that maybe their son had returned from Australia to check on the house.'

Kurt McDonald, Carlson thought, continuing to make notes.

'Rebecca, what is the name of the street that the McDonalds' house is on?'

'Well,' replied Rebecca, 'the street no longer exists but it was called Cudthy Street.'

Anneka typed the name into the computer on the desk she had taken over. Bearing in mind Rebecca's words that the street no longer existed, she decided to check the search date terms from the 1950s. *If they bought the house in the 1960s then Cudthy Street will be there.* She watched while the computer loaded itself. A map appeared on screen, the very same ordnance survey map of the area from 1954.

A red cursor appeared over a small street with the name 'Cudthy'.

'Thank you, Rebecca,' Anneka said. 'What happened to Cudthy Street?'

'My mum told me that the street used to run parallel to the McDonalds' house but the main street and the rest of the buildings that were on it disappeared just before 1990, as a result of the local council clearing space for green-belt land. The McDonalds didn't lose their house, however, because the size of their land meant that they were to benefit.'

'To benefit in what way?' asked Carlson.

'Because,' said Rebecca, 'they got to keep the massive site of their own land and the rest of the street vanished, which meant that their plot became even bigger. It's virtually a forest growing out in all directions from that house now.'

Carlson thanked Rebecca Mayfield and promised that somebody would contact her again in the course of their investigations to let her know how it was progressing.

She stood up and gave the desk and phone back to the young constable who had been hovering in the vicinity. She headed back to where Buzan was sitting, thinking about the information she had just discovered. As she approached his desk, she called out to him, 'Fuz, I have good news. I know who Geraldine Lopez was.'

He looked up as she pulled up a seat.

'I've just spoken to the cops in Australia, a helpful inspector called Stamatis. It's not a case of who Geraldine Lopez *was* but who she *is*. Stamatis told me that she lives somewhere in the outback and as it's getting late there they'll have to wait until tomorrow morning to send an officer out to see her.'

'Good work,' replied Anneka. 'I just finished speaking with a woman by the name of Rebecca Mayfield. She claims that the McDonalds were neighbours of her family. Apparently her mother knew Maria McDonald quite well.'

'What else did she tell you?' asked Buzan.

'As far as she knows, the family did move to Australia in 1996. After they left, her mother received a letter from Maria McDonald stating that she and her family had gone specifically to Australia because, in her ailing years, she wanted to be close to her family and, more specifically, her sister – Geraldine.'

'So that's the relationship between Maria and Geraldine,' said Buzan.

'More interesting than that, however, is that William McDonald did indeed lie about the name of the street he lived in. It wasn't called Dutchy Street at all. It was actually called Cudthy Street and the whole street except the McDonalds' house disappeared just prior to 1990 as a result of some kind of governmental green-belt scheme.'

Buzan contemplated her words.

'That would make sense. The green-belt thing, I mean. Plus the most recent map we saw was from 1988, prior to the time of the green-belt development.'

'Yep,' agreed Anneka. Her face grew pointedly more serious. 'We need to speak to Inspector Roberts as soon as possible. Rebecca Mayfield claims that she has seen activity around the vicinity of the McDonalds' old house. She assumed that the son, Kurt, has been back over from Australia, regularly checking on the family home. We need to get over to that house, Fuz.'

Monday 10 October, 10 p.m., Sunset Creek, Brisbane, Queensland, Australia

Geraldine Lopez was the youngest of Maria Lopez's siblings. Her sister Maria had been born twenty-five years before her and had been the oldest of five brothers and sisters, all of whom were now deceased. Geraldine didn't quite resent having only seen her oldest sister briefly in her life, but she did feel troubled when she thought of her only nephew, Kurt, living alone in England. He had informed her of her sister's death from multiple sclerosis in 1996 and she had been making her best efforts since that time to stay in touch with him. She wasn't getting any younger herself.

She had decided, upon the death of her sister, to continue making payments into her bank account, for Kurt's sake. She had often wondered why he remained so elusive and seemingly uninterested in his family in Australia. *The least I can do is send him some money every month,* she had thought. She did, after all, have a large fortune that her parents had bequeathed to her and her siblings upon their death. Her grandparents had been early settlers in Australia and had worked hard to build up a substantial family wealth from gold-mining. They had started much like other now-gold-rich families who had been the product of migration. Panning, sluicing, dredging, cradling and finally hard-rock mining had brought them a substantial income over the decades.

Now, with her retirement years approaching fast and with no children of her own, she had been making extra efforts to reach out to her nephew in England. His correspondence had been infrequent and Geraldine couldn't help but feel an uneasy nagging in the back of her mind, telling her that this was a man who only made contact when he wanted something. She had tried to brush these thoughts aside for the sake of her late sister's memory.

Why did he sometimes post her documents, already sealed and addressed for delivery back to the UK? She had thought it may be that he didn't want contact with certain people and wanted them kept at bay from his life. Apparently it was quite common that people with family overseas would send such requests. Kurt had never shared with his auntie the reasons why he made such requests from her. She had, over the years, just accepted them as an odd quirk of his personality.

Chapter Eighteen

Detective Inspector James Roberts and Dr Karen Laos had made good time on their trip back to Manchester. They had been updated with the progress that Detective Constables Buzan and Carlson had made with regard to the bank accounts and the Australian connection to William and Maria McDonald. Now, fifteen minutes out of Manchester's city centre, Karen Laos was reviewing her notepad. She had written *'Dutchy Street'* and circled it and alongside it she had written the correct name of *'Cudthy Street'*.

'James?' she said.

He glanced at her.

'Don't you think that Dutchy and Cudthy are remarkably similar names?' she asked.

'Similar,' he said.

Karen took out her pen once more and started playing with the letters.

Inspector Roberts checked his watch and their current location. 'We should be back at the station within ten minutes,' he said.

'And what's the plan for when we get there?' asked Karen.

'That depends,' he replied, 'on whether Aled Bevan manages to find the letters that his grandmother says she received from Maria McDonald. Either way we will have to get over to this Manor House in Cudthy Street.' He shrugged his shoulders and added, 'Or what's left of it.'

He knew that any police raid would have to be carefully planned and executed in such dense greenery and forestry. He was sure that the detective chief inspector was already working on such planning and contingencies. Before they got back to the police station, however, there was something else he wanted to talk to Karen about.

He shifted in his seat. Karen knew what was coming. *His body language is the same as it was back in the hotel,* she thought.

'Karen. Before we get back to the station, can we talk about what happened last night?'

They hadn't discussed it at all during the course of the day.

'James, please, don't say any more,' replied Karen. 'I don't want to simply brush it off as a drunken escapade. But on the same count, I don't want to talk about future plans. Can we just see where it goes and be friends?"

James thought briefly about her response. A sense of relief flowed through his body. Part of him did long for a relationship; another part was terrified at the prospect. *Much like Karen.*

He reached out and took Karen's hand.

'Friends,' he said, quickly adding, 'Friends that are going to see what happens.'

As Karen smiled at him, his mobile phone started to

vibrate on the dashboard. He asked Karen to pick it up for him.

An email indicated that a fax had been automatically forwarded by the police exchange server. Karen checked the screen of the phone.

'It's a match,' she said.

'What is?' asked James.

'Cudthy Street. Aled found his grandmother's letters. It's the same name exactly.'

'That means,' said James excitedly, 'that everything matches. All evidence is pointing us to this Manor House.'

Roberts thought about their journey so far. *The hydrogen peroxide that William McDonald had purchased from Dr Jackson's business; the age of it was a match with the H_2O_2 found on both victims. The wool and subsequent yarn from the Balween, traced from Brecon, Wales and all the way back to Rochdale. The mysterious disappearance of the McDonald family to Australia and yet no records to confirm the same. The McDonalds' neighbour who had given Maria McDonald such a large supply of clonazepam.*

All of these were reasons enough for the police to raid Manor House. Karen shocked Roberts out of his thoughts.

'That's it!' she exclaimed. 'Dutchy Street is simply an anagram of Cudthy Street.'

She looked pleased with her conclusion, a pen in her right hand and her notebook now annotated with several markings.

'That certainly explains why Anneka and Buzan were dumbfounded by the maps. There never was such a street as Dutchy,' said Roberts.

*

Monday 10 October, 1.30 p.m.,
Greater Manchester Police Headquarters

Detective Inspector James Roberts and Dr Karen Laos walked into a busy conference room over which Detective Chief Inspector Morti presided. This was an ears and eyes-only conference for those closest to the investigation. That is, it was meant to be. However, with the media having upped the pressure since the previous day's press conference, headlines had appeared in the local media, with runner-lines such as *'Peroxide Killer Returns to Taunt Manchester'* and *'The Peroxide Homicide Child Killer is Back'*.

Morti had decided to give full authority to his officers to launch a raid on Manor House in Cudthy Street. He walked up and down in front of his assembled colleagues, behind him a large map of Rochdale with red marker dots indicating the approach that the team would take. He had invited Special Branch officers from the firearms squad for tactical advice. They stood, unmistakably grim, at the back of the room, watching the proceedings.

'Welcome back,' he said to Inspector Robert and Dr Laos as they found seats.

Detective Inspector James Roberts looked up at his superior to acknowledge his welcome. Morti continued pacing back and forth in front of his colleagues. He paused, centre of the room, one hand tucked into the top of his trousers, the other ready to point at the map and board behind him.

'Officers, ladies and gentlemen,' he started. 'We have a confirmed link to the house in Rochdale as a result of two investigations that have been running parallel to one another.'

He pointed at Roberts and Karen Laos.

'Detective Inspector Roberts and Dr Laos have been able

to confirm the origins of the wool yarn found in which both victims were dressed as having originated from a farm in Brecon, in Wales. They have also confirmed that the wool was purchased by an Edna McDonald, who was the mother of William McDonald. They have also confirmed that William McDonald purchased large quantities of hydrogen peroxide from Dr Joan Jackson's company in the early 1990s. Dr Laos has been able to determine that the age of the substance found on both victims is consistent with hydrogen peroxide that would have been purchased at approximately that time.'

He looked over at Detective Constables Carlson and Buzan. It was their turn for the pointed finger.

'Detective Constable Carlson and Detective Constable Buzan have been able to speak to a neighbour of the McDonalds, by the name of Rebecca Mayfield, who claims that the McDonald family moved to Australia in 1996. This is consistent with the governmental census that William McDonald apparently sent from Australia back to the UK a few months after the family moved. Therefore, we don't know what we will find when we visit Manor House. Rebecca Mayfield told Detective Constable Carlson that her mother, Cecily Mayfield, now deceased, gave a large quantity of the drug clonazepam to William McDonald. The neighbour also states that it is possible that the son of the McDonalds, Kurt McDonald is, or has been, visiting the family house in Rochdale.

'Therefore, until the police in Australia determine from Maria McDonald's sister, Geraldine Lopez, whether the McDonald family did indeed move to Australia in 1996, we have to assume that they did. We can also assume that the main suspect we are now looking for is their son, Kurt McDonald.'

His face changed and a more serious expression replaced his previously animated one.

'For that reason I have asked our colleagues from firearms to join the raid.'

He looked over at the armed officers and then turned towards the map behind him.

'We will approach the house from three directions. Detective Inspector Roberts, I want you to join the armed officers. You will head that team. You will approach the house from this direction.'

He pointed at a location on the map that showed an expanse of green-belt land approximately two miles wide, which would lead the team directly from the south into the gardens of Manor House. Detective Inspector Roberts nodded. Dr Laos gave him a concerned glance.

'The second team,' continued the detective chief inspector, 'will be led by Detective Constable Carlson, who will be joined by uniformed officers.

'Detective Constable Carlson. I know that you are not a firearms officer but you will of course be dressed in bullet-proof clothing, as will the rest of your team. You will all be equipped with standard protective equipment, including pepper sprays and batons. You will also carry shields at all times. Your team will head towards the house from this direction.'

He indicated at the map, his finger tracing a route that would take Detective Constable Carlson and her colleagues from the north, through a mile of green-belt land.

'Your team will depart twenty minutes after Detective Inspector Roberts' team,' he said. 'This will allow enough time for Detective Inspector Roberts and the firearms officers to be on the site of the house before your team arrive.

'Finally,' continued Morti, 'additional teams will be posted at all known exits from the area around the house. A police helicopter will also be in the vicinity in case air-to-ground coordination is required.'

He looked at all of his colleagues.

'We have to assume that Kurt McDonald, if he's at the house, is armed and dangerous. He is the only suspect we have in this case. If he is the person we're looking for, we know that he has already killed twice that we know of and he is therefore very likely to be able to do so again. Get your teams ready and get moving within the next thirty minutes.'

The room started to empty. Karen took Inspector Roberts' hand.

'Be careful out there, James,' she urged.

'I will be, don't worry,' he said. 'I'll see you later.'

He stood up and walked away to join his team of firearms officers. Dr Laos watched them depart the room.

Chapter Nineteen

Monday 10 October, 3 p.m.,
Manor House, Rochdale

Kurt McDonald moved into a position in his cellar from where he could see his trophies. Several jars sat on high shelves against the walls, the keep-sakes from his victims' bodies. He was particularly impressed by the way in which his latest prop's tonsils now sat dynamic, loved and preserved in solution. He felt that he had pleased Abeona over the last six years.

He wanted to give her the gift that was his victims so that she would protect and guide them for eternity. He knew that his work would help to fulfil a better purpose. Without him, his props would have faced the same hardship that he himself had endured through his own childhood. *If only someone had helped me in the same way I helped them.* He often thought along these lines when in a contemplative mood. *Abeona saved me and now she has the souls of her children to save.*

Kurt knew that Abeona would only ask for his help once every six years and only during the month of October. The books he had found in the local library after his parents had died had told him that. Abeona had been neglected by the world until he had called out her name for the first time when he was seventeen, the year after he had killed his parents. Her coming was almost complete. He felt his purpose and mission more keenly than ever before.

Monday 10 October, 3.25 p.m., Manor House, Rochdale

Detective Inspector James Roberts and his team had cleared the first mile of the thick undergrowth that formed the length of the green-belt area. Dressed in full police gear with shield and helmet, Roberts cast his mind back to his training. Today, he had his Heckler & Koch MP5 semi-automatic in a shoulder strap, the safety lock engaged. He had been taught only to shoot when all other options had been exhausted.

If you shoot, shoot to incapacitate in the first instance. If your life is threatened, or a life of one of your colleagues or a member of the public is in danger, shoot to kill. The words had been imprinted into his mind.

From his position at the front of the team he could see a large foreboding house looming out from between the forest. *Manor House,* he told himself. He stopped and indicated the house to the firearms officers that followed him. They were spread in a standard diamond pattern, spanning out to a maximum of four metres on all sides. Inspector Roberts shifted his direction to get a better view of the house. The other officers in his team followed his lead. They headed deeper into the extensive undergrowth. The ground was waterlogged, the sky full of threatening rain.

Inspector Roberts knew that he and his team had to

secure the site before Detective Constable Carlson's team arrived at the house.

The house came into clearer view as he moved forward, in stealth-mode, his firearms training coming back to him as he moved along, closer to his target. They had now cleared the green-belt land and Detective Inspector Roberts looked in all directions, assessing the size of the land that Manor House stood on. Forensic psychologist Trevor Stephenson had been correct about the isolation that this type of offender would both desire and require.

Several neglected and rotting sheds and buildings made of wood were visible ahead and he could now see the large house clearly. They had approached through the under-growth and come out at the back of the house. The team paused; Roberts indicated with his hands where he wanted them to go. He decided to keep the group together rather than split up. A tactical decision. They followed his directions and came up on one of the falling structures that constituted an outhouse.

Detective Inspector Roberts moved in first, slowly, his Heckler & Koch now in his hand. He moved sharply against the outer wall, keenly scanning the area with his eyes. He saw a door hanging off its hinges, indicating the entrance. He pushed forward whilst one of the officers with him moved along the far side of the building's perimeter, checking for exits. He returned, confirming that there were none. *One door, both the entrance and the exit.*

The team formed a line behind Detective Inspector Roberts as he entered the building. They spanned out in a triangular pattern, covering all corners of the building, each indicating 'clear' as they checked their own areas. Detective Inspector Roberts saw little in the building of interest.

A few falling tables and some empty flower pots, long past their best. He moved cautiously through the building and saw three large plastic drums, which he assumed housed McDonald's hydrogen peroxide. With a quick and steady hand motion, he told his team to exit the building.

Monday 10 October, 4 p.m., Manor House, Rochdale

Detective Constable Carlson and her team had cleared a mile of green-belt land and found themselves in full sight of the north side of Manor House. They lowered their position as the undergrowth here was relatively poor. Carlson felt a shudder of excitement as she looked at the house. She had a full uninterrupted view of the large building.

She looked at the windows and saw no sign of life inside. The large front door was close to what she might describe as being infirm, much like the rest of the house. She had her police radio tapped into a wireless headset and had heard nothing from Detective Inspector Roberts or his team. She set the frequency to one that would allow her to speak to the rest of her team without interrupting the detective inspector.

'We'll wait here until we hear from Inspector Roberts and his team,' she said quietly into her mouthpiece.

The uniformed officers with her did not respond verbally. She looked at them all individually to ensure that they had heard her. Each returned her stare in turn, indicating that they had understood her clearly. They waited in position.

*

Monday 10 October, 4.15 p.m.,
Manor House, Rochdale

As Detective Inspector Roberts and his team came closer to
the back of Manor House, they paused, hearing the sound of
a police helicopter in the distance, which had not yet come
into vision. *Better that way,* Roberts told himself. He didn't
want the noise of a great big helicopter scaring away their
only suspect if he were in the house. Using both his arms, he
indicated to the rest of his team that he wanted them to fan
out in a U-shape as they approached what seemed to be the
back door of the house.

They fanned out, Detective Inspector Roberts heading
up the front of the group, his gun still in his hand. He was
flanked to the left, right and the rear by armed officers. He
felt his heartbeat increase and the adrenaline pump as he
reached out to try the handle of the back door. It was open.
He pushed gently and the door swung inwards into a large
kitchen. It was as neglected as the grounds of the house.

Detective Inspector Roberts entered first, again with his
back flat to the first wall he came across. He moved along,
signalling for his colleagues to follow. He heard no sounds.
The kitchen smelt damp and mouldy. The setting inside
mirrored that of the outside; the place looked abandoned. As
he looked into the hallway leading off the main kitchen, he
was reminded of Miss Havisham's house in Charles Dickens'
Great Expectations.

The light outside had started rapidly disappearing into
the autumnal evening. Detective Inspector Roberts knew
that he had to act before they lost the light completely. As he
approached the door leading to the hallway, he found himself
doing a double-take, suddenly surprised to see a crack of dim

light emanating up from below the kitchen floor. He followed the light with his eyes and spotted a trapdoor leading down beneath the house.

He let his team know with the move of his right arm, pointing downwards towards the floor. One of the armed officers moved quietly to the reverse side of the trapdoor and reached down. He lifted it slowly, a dark-yellow light making its way up into the kitchen. Detective Inspector Roberts decided the time was right to make their presence known.

'Kurt McDonald!' he called, loud enough for anyone within a range of ten metres to hear.

There was no response.

He called again.

'Kurt McDonald. This is Detective Inspector Roberts. I am here with other police officers. Please let us know if you are here. You should know that we are armed.'

Always give the suspect the chance to surrender. The words from his training came back to him from a distant place in his past. Again, there was no response. Roberts could see no other sign of artificial light coming from anywhere in the house. He decided to take his chances and move down into the cellar. He took one step at a time, directly behind one of his armed colleagues. *Two guns; his and the firearm officer's.*

The other officers waited in the kitchen, one facing in towards the trapdoor, the others facing out, keeping watch for any sign of movement in the rest of the house. As Detective Inspector Roberts stepped down to the last rung of the ladder steps, he felt the force and speed of a train crashing directly into his abdomen.

Kurt McDonald had come fast and furious against him with the thick short end of a plank of wood. He hit Roberts squarely in the stomach, sent him flying down the last step and falling, winded, onto the cold concrete floor beneath. Roberts managed to look up as he saw McDonald lunging at him again.

He rolled out of the way and then, in slow motion, saw his armed colleague swinging at the back of McDonald's legs with his heavy baton. McDonald let out a sharp scream of pain as he too went crashing down onto the floor. The armed officer quickly jumped onto his back and pulled McDonald's arms up in a form of restraint. McDonald was strong and tried to squirm free.

Detective Inspector Roberts took a deep breath, his body still struggling to suck air into his lungs, his mind reeling from the sudden and quick action. The pain was deep and powerful. He saw his colleague struggling and unclipped the handcuffs he had on his belt.

He shuffled his painful body to where his colleague was struggling to keep McDonald on the floor and reached out and cuffed McDonald's hands together, forcing out the standard police arrest blurb.

'Kurt McDonald, I am arresting you on suspicion of murder. You do not have to say anything. However, it may harm your defence if you do not mention when questioned something which you later rely on in court. Anything you do say may be given in evidence.'

He then crumpled back to a seated position, his back against the steps that he had so brutally been forced off. He lifted his radio, panting, and spoke into the device.

'Roberts to all units. The suspect has been apprehended. Repeat, the suspect has been apprehended.'

A short second later he heard Detective Constable Carlson's voice respond.

'What is your location sir?'

He answered as the rest of his team made their way down the steps.

He heard the sound of the police helicopter closing in on the grounds of Manor House and watched as three of his burly colleagues lifted McDonald clean off his feet and dragged him up the stairs. It was then that Detective Inspector Roberts, for the first time since his undignified fall, looked around the cellar. It was massive. His face dropped as he saw the jars lining the walls. He instinctively knew what their contents would be. *Get the hell out of here, James,* he told himself. *Crime scene can sort this mess out. Your job is done.*

Chapter Twenty

Thursday 13 October, 10 a.m.,
Lloyd's Coffee Shop, Manchester

Dr Karen Laos had asked to meet Detective Inspector
Roberts this morning; it was the first time she would have
seen him since Monday's events. She had ordered him a caffé
latte, which she knew was his favourite type of coffee. He had
been busy with police reports and attending to the media,
who were running with the story every hour of every day. The
peroxide homicide murderer had been caught and, best of all
for the press, he wasn't just a killer, but a serial killer.

The discovery of Kurt McDonald's decomposed father's
remains in the white oak cask of whisky and the discovery
of his late mother's bones in the garden, under the downy
birch, officially made McDonald a serial killer. His auntie in
Australia had understandably been horrified to learn of her
nephew's actions. She had been fully cooperative with the
police in Australia, explaining that she thought her sister
and her husband had died of natural causes.

She had no idea that the envelopes she had been posting
back to the UK were actually Kurt's way of fooling the system

into thinking his parents – and he himself – had moved to Australia. Manor House had been seized by the police and the forensic psychologist Trevor Stephenson was busy with SOCO, checking every square inch of the house and forming a completed profile of the killer now in their custody.

He had been remanded temporarily into a high-secure psychiatric facility for mental health examination, although nobody thought he was clinically insane. The prosecution were planning to argue that this man was a psychopath and as such should be jailed in a regular prison rather than a facility for the mentally ill. Kurt McDonald had said nothing since his arrest, other than to confirm his name.

Karen thought about all that had unfolded as she sat waiting for James to arrive. She looked up and saw him coming in through the front door. She stood up and they greeted one another with a hug.

'So, how's it going down at the station?' she asked.

James smiled at her. 'Are you missing being a cop, Karen?' he asked.

'No, not at all,' she replied with a small laugh.

'It's going fine, all considered,' he said. 'Thanks for all your hard work.'

Karen held his gaze before replying. 'It was my pleasure to work with you again, James.'

'As it was mine,' he said. He picked up his coffee. 'I guess you're pleased to be back at the mortuary again?'

'I don't know if *pleased* is the right word,' Karen replied, sipping her coffee. 'But yes. I am comfortable being back on routine cases. In fact, I have spoken to my superiors and they suggested I take a holiday.'

She said the words with a kind of delight that James found infectious.

'And did you agree to taking a holiday?' he asked.

'As a matter of fact, I did,' Karen replied. 'I'm off from today for the next two weeks and after this coffee I'm heading off to the travel agent.'

Detective Inspector Roberts looked at her and couldn't help but ask. 'Do you want company?'

'To walk to the travel agent?' teased Karen.

'I meant on your holiday. You know, as two *friends* together.'

'I know what you meant,' she said. 'If you can get the time, I would be thrilled to have you join me.'

James pulled out his mobile and called Detective Chief Inspector Philip Morti. It was a quick call, which told Karen that his leave had been immediately approved. They finished their coffees.

As they stood up, James took her hand.

'So, Dr Laos, where are we going?'

'I thought the Caribbean would be nice this time of year,' she said as they left the coffee shop and walked out into the morning drizzle of a busy Manchester shopping street.